'In two earlier bo
us to Harold She
inconsistent magi
legend which he reaches using
stories are gems of fantasy and have had numerous editions, but THE ENCHANTER COMPLEATED†, the last in the series . . . had only a single book edition (1960) after its original magazine appearance and became a collector's item. Now with this welcome new edition we can all once again enjoy the adventures of Harold and his wife Belphebe (from Spenser's 'Faerie Queene') as they muddle their way across the worlds of Finnish and Irish legend . . . charming fun'–*Publishers' Weekly*

**The Incompleat Enchanter* and *The Castle of Iron* (both available in Sphere Books).

†Published in the United States of America under the title *Wall of Serpents*.

Also by L. Sprague de Camp in Sphere Books

LEST DARKNESS FALL
THE FALLIBLE FIEND
THE TRITONIAN RING
THE GOBLIN TOWER
THE CLOCKS OF IRAZ
THE INCOMPLEAT ENCHANTER (with Fletcher Pratt)
THE CASTLE OF IRON (with Fletcher Pratt)
CONAN THE USURPER
CONAN THE FREEBOOTER (with Lin Carter)
CONAN OF CIMMERIA (with Robert E. Howard and Lin Carter)
CONAN THE WANDERER (with Lin Carter)
CONAN THE BUCCANEER (with Lin Carter)
CONAN OF THE ISLES (with Lin Carter)
CONAN OF AQUILONIA (with Lin Carter)
CONAN THE SWORDSMAN (with Lin Carter)
CONAN THE LIBERATOR (with Lin Carter)

The Enchanter Compleated

L. Sprague de Camp & Fletcher Pratt
Foreword by Catherine Crook de Camp

SPHERE BOOKS LIMITED
30/32 Gray's Inn Road, London WC1X 8JL

First published in Great Britain in 1980 by Sphere Books Ltd

TRADE
MARK

Set in Times
Printed in Great Britain by
William Collins Sons & Co Ltd
Glasgow.

Foreword

Readers familiar with the genre of literature known as heroic fantasy, or sword-and-sorcery stories, are aware that its roots lie in late nineteenth-century England. Long before these action-packed fantastic tales received a name, they were being penned by British writers such as William Morris and Lord Dunsany; and, in the first half of the present century, by E. R. Eddison and the master of heroic fantasy J. R. R. Tolkien.

Although Edgar Rice Burroughs with his novel *A Princess of Mars* (1917) and his other John Carter stories might be considered a precursor, the real founder of the genre in America was Robert E. Howard, a gifted young Texan. In the early 1930s, Howard created CONAN, the mighty barbarian who bestrode an ancient continent with unsheathed sword and fought his way to kingship.

Heroic fantasy was still unnamed in 1938 when Tolkien brought out his children's book. *The Hobbit.* Although it was an instant success, both in England and in the United States, his more ambitious adult fantasy trilogy, *Lord of the Rings*, received little acclaim when, in 1945, a hardcover edition was published in America. Only when a paperbound reprint appeared ten years later did the work rise like a rocket into the ranks of all-time best sellers, where both it and the final Tolkien work, *The Silmarillion*, remain to this day.

Perhaps less well-known is the fact that, a few years after Robert E. Howard's death, a pair of authors. L. Sprague de Camp (1907–) and Fletcher Pratt (1897–1956) working in collaboration, became outstanding early creators of heroic fantasy in America.

(Murray) Fletcher Pratt came from a background far removed from that of his younger collaborator. Son of an upstate New York farmer, he was born on an Indian

Reservation near Buffalo. As a high school student, this pint-sized youth – five foot three – became a prizefighter in the flyweight class. He also held a job as a librarian in the local public library, only to find that the head librarian disapproved of an employee who was a professional fighter.

After a year at Hobart College, at Geneva, New York, Pratt had to leave school for lack of money. He worked as a newspaper reporter and spent a year in Paris with his second wife Inga Stevens Pratt, before settling down in New York to a life of free-lance writing.

As a young writer, Pratt held several fringe jobs. One was translating foreign science fiction stories for the publisher of *Wonder Stories*, Hugo Gernsback. When Mr Gernsback failed to pay him as promised, Pratt would withhold the final chapters of the novel or story he was translating until the publisher ran out of stalling time and paid him what was owed.

As the years passed, Fletcher Pratt became a self-taught scholar of considerable attainments. He hit his stride with a distinguished book about the War of 1812, *The Heroic Years*, and a popular history of the American Civil War, *Ordeal by Fire*. A man of many interests and an extraordinary sense of fun, Pratt and his wife surrounded themselves with cages full of squealing marmosets and a never-ending stream of friends and visitors.

L. Sprague de Camp, born in New York City, was educated in private schools there in the South and in California. He attended California Institute of Technology, earning his degree in Aeronautical Engineering in 1930, and took his Master's in Economics from Stevens Institute of Technology in 1933.

De Camp's post-college years were spent as an engineer in the Adirondacks, a patent expert, and a lieutenant-commander in the United States Naval Reserve during the Second World War. Stationed in Philadelphia at the Air Materials Centre, he, Robert Heinlein and Issac Asimov fought the war with flashing slide rules, and with their wives spent weekends together whenever their gasoline ration permitted.

In 1938, several years before coming to Philadelphia, Sprague de Camp met Fletcher Pratt when a mutual friend, John D. Clark, brought him around to one of Pratt's famous naval war games. The Pratts were then living in a groundfloor apartment with a small garden in a remodelled brownstone house in the West 20s. Once or twice a month, the Pratts would invite all and sundry to spend an evening crawling around on hands and knees, moving model warships into range of 'enemy ships'. Then all players would relax with a glass of beer while umpires painstakingly measured the distances, marked the damage to the ships, and removed 'sunken' vessels from the parquet floor.

From this strange beginning, a lifetime friendship grew; and Fletcher invited Sprague – then just starting his literary career – to collaborate on several tales in which the hero won the day by means of his agile brain, rather than by his bulging thews. The results of this collaboration were two individual novels. *The Land of Unreason* (1942) and *The Carnelian Cube* (1948) and a series of five stories written between 1941 and 1950 about the adventures of Harold Shea, a brash young psychologist who finds himself in a succession of fantasy worlds where magic works and magical formulae can be worked out with mathematical precision, if only one has the head for figures.

In the first of these novels, 'The Roaring Trumpet', the unheroic hero finds himself in the world of Norse mythology during the twilight of the gods. In the second. 'The Mathematics of Magic', Shea's boss, Dr Chalmers, and a friend, Walter Bayard, join the peripatetic psychologist on a jaunt into the midst of Spenser's *Faerie Queene*. Soon thereafter, Harold Shea's adventures continue in 'The Castle of Iron', during his visit to the chivalrous cosmos of Ariosto's Italian verse romance *Orlando Furioso*.

When these stories appeared in *Unknown* in 1940 and 1941, they received such wide acclaim that the first two were shortly published by Henry Holt as a book entitled

The Incompleat Enchanter.

Spurred by this success, de Camp and Pratt wrote two more Harold Shea tales. The first, 'The Wall of Serpents,' appeared in June 1953 in a short-lived publication called *Fantasy Fiction:* the second, 'The Green Magician', was published in *Beyond Fantasy Fiction,* Number Nine, October 1954. In the first story, Shea explores the world of Finnish myth; while the second takes him to the emerald isle of Irish legend. These final stories of the series were brought out as *Wall of Serpents* in a 1500-copy edition, published by Avalon Press in 1960.

Although in 1975 Ballantine gathered together the first three tales of Shea's adventures under the somewhat misleading title *The Compleat Enchanter*, the remaining two have for a quarter of a century been unobtainable by all save a few well-heeled collectors. It is, therefore, for the enjoyment of a whole new generation of readers that Phantasia Press prepared this edition of *Wall of Serpents*, a book which might have borne the title *The Enchanter Compleated**. Readers may be interested to learn that all five tales are presently being published in England, Germany and Italy.

10 May 1978 Catherine Crook de Camp

* And does in this Sphere Books edition.

One

The mail was neatly stacked on the table in the front hall. Belphebe said, 'Mrs Dambrot is having cocktails on the fifteenth. That's Thurday, isn't it? And here's a note for the maid, poor wretch. The Morrisons are having a lawn party Sunday and want us to come. This one's really for you; it's from that McCarthy wittold who was in your class last semester, and he wants to know when he can call on us and talk about ps-psionics.'

'Oh, that,' said Harold Shea. He pushed back his black hair and stroked his long nose.

'And will we subscribe five dollars to the Guild for . . .'

'Hell!' said Shea.

She cocked her head to one side, eyeing him from under arched brows. He thought how pretty she was and how remarkably she had adapted herself to his own space-time continuum since he had brought her from the universe of the *Faerie Queen*, and later rescued her from that of the *Orlando Furioso*, whither his collaborator Chalmers had accidentally snatched her while angling for Shea to help him out of a private predicament.

'My most sweet lord,' she said, 'I do protest you want in courtesy. When you cozened me to wed with you, 'twas with fair promise that my life would be a very paradise.'

He slipped an arm around her and kissed her before she could dodge. 'Life anywhere with you would be a paradise. But lawn parties! And the home for homeless poodles, five dollars!'

Belphebe laughed. 'The Morrisons are gentle folk. There will be lemonade and little sandwiches. And we shall probably play charades, 'stead of being pursued by barbarous Moors.'

Shea seized her by both shoulders and looked intently at the expression of wide-eyed innocence she had assumed.

'If I didn't know you better, kid, I'd say you were trying to persuade me to get out of it somehow, but getting me to make the proposition. Just like a woman.'

'My most dear lord! I am but a dutiful wife, that loves but to do her husband's will.'

'When it's the same as your own, you mean. All right. Ohio bores you. But you don't want to go back to Castle Carena and that gang of tinplated thugs, do you? We never did find out who won the magical duel, Atlantes or Astolph.'

'Not I. But come, sir, let us reason together on this.' She led the way into the living-room and sat down. 'In serious sooth, though we are but newly returned and though this Ohio be a land of smiling peace and good order, I think we too lightly promised each other to wander no more.'

'You mean,' said Shea, 'that you can take only so much peace and good order? I can't say I blame you. Doc Chalmers used to tell me I should have taken to politics or become a soldier of fortune instead of a psychologist, and damned if . . .'

'It is not solely that whereon I think,' she said. 'Have you any word further on your friends who were lately with us?'

'I haven't checked today, but none of them had come back yesterday.'

She looked worried. In the course of their incursion into the continuum of Ariosto's *Orlando* epics, they had left no less than four colleagues and innocent bystanders scattered about sundry universes. 'That were a week complete since our return.'

'Yes,' said Shea. 'I don't know that I blame Doc Chalmers and Vaclav Polacek for staying in the world of the *Orlando Furioso* – they were having a good time there. But Walter Bayard and Pete the cop were stuck in Coleridge's Xanadu the last I know, and I don't think they were having a very good time. Doc was supposed to send them back here, and he either couldn't make it or forgot.'

Belphebe said: 'And there are those who would take it amiss if they did not come? Even as you have told me that the police sought you out when I was missing in the land of Castle Carena?'

'I'll say so. Especially since one of them is a cop. In this land of peace and good order it's a lot more dangerous to monkey with a policeman than with a professor.'

She looked down and moved one hand on the edge of the couch. 'I feared as much . . . Harold.'

'What's the matter, kid?'

'There is a kind of knowledge we woodlings have that those in the cities do not know. When I went abroad today, I was followed both here and there without once being able to see by whom or for what purpose.'

Shea leaped up. 'Why, the dirty skunks! I'll . . .'

'No, Harold. Be not so fiery-fierce. Could you not go to them and tell them the simple truth?'

'They wouldn't believe it any more than they did the last time. And if they did, it might start a mass migration to other space-time continua. No, thanks. Even Doc Chalmers hasn't worked out all the rules of transfer yet, and it all might turn out to be as dangerous as selling atomic bombs in department stores.'

Belphebe cupped her chin in one hand. 'Aye. I do recall how we were ejected from my own dear land of Faerie, never to return, in spite of your symbolic logic that changes all impressions the senses do receive. Yet I like the present prospect but little.' She referred to Shea's final desperate spell in his conflict with the wizard Dolon. Dolon had been destroyed, but Shea had worked up so much magical potential that he had been thrown back into his own universe, dragging Belphebe with him.

Belphebe's brows went up. 'Never before have I known you so lacking in resource. Or is it that you do not wish to go? Hark! – is there not some frame of thought, some world to which we could remove and find a magic strong enough to overcome this of Xanadu? Thus we might outflank our trouble rather than essaying to beat it down by assault direct.'

Shea noticed that she was assuming the question of whether she should accompany him to be settled, but he had now been married long enough to know better than to make an issue of it.

'It's an idea, anyway. Hmm, maybe Arthurian Britain. No – all the magicians there are bad eggs except Bleys and Merlin. Bleys is pretty feeble, and Merlin we couldn't be sure of finding, since he spends a lot of time in our own continuum.' (Merlin had put in an appearance in the final scene of their Orlandian adventure.) 'The *Iliad* and *Odyssey* haven't any professionals except Circe, and she was a pretty tough baby, not likely to help either of us. There aren't any magicians to speak of in *Siegfried* or *Beowulf* . . . Wait a minute, I think I've got it. The *Kalevala*!'

'What might that be?'

'The Finnish epic. Practically all the big shots in it are magicians and poets, too. Vainamoinen could be a big help – "Vainamoinen, old and steadfast . . ." A guy with a heart the size of a balloon. But we'll need some equipment if we go there. I'll need a sword, and you had better take a knife and a good bow. The party might get rough.'

Belphebe glowed. 'That lovely bow of the alloy of magnesium, with the sight, that lately I used in the contest for the championship of Ohio?'

'N-no, I think not. It probably wouldn't work in the Finnish frame of reference. Might turn brittle and snap or something. Better use the old wooden one. And wooden arrows, too. None of these machine-age steel things you're so crazy about.'

She asked, 'If this Finland be where I think, will it not be uncomfortable cold?'

'You bet. None of that perpetual summer you had in Faerie. I've got enough backwoods clothes to do me, and I'll make out a list for you. This sounds like a breeches-and-boots expedition.'

'What kind of country would it be?'

'Near as I can make out, it's one vast sub-arctic swamp. A flat land covered by dense forest, with little lakes everywhere.'

'Then,' she said, 'boots of rubber would serve us well.'

Shea shook his head. 'Nothing doing. For the same reason that you shouldn't take that trick magnesium bow. No rubber in this mental pattern. I made that mistake among the Norse gods and nearly got my ears beaten off for it.'

'But . . .'

'Listen, take my word for it. Leather boots, laced and well greased. Wool shirts, leather jackets, gloves . . . you'd better get a pair of those mittens that leave one finger free. After we get there, we can get some native clothes. Here's the list – oh, yes, woollen underwear. And drive slow, see?'

He looked at her as sternly as he could manage. Belphebe had a tendency to drive the Shea Chevrolet as though she were piloting a jet fighter.

'Oh, I'll be a very model of prudence.' She shifted from foot to foot.

'And while you're gone,' he continued, 'I'll get out the symbol-cards and grease up our syllogismobile.'

When Belphebe returned two hours later, Harold Shea was squatting cross-legged on his living-room floor with the cards laid out in front of him. They looked something like the Zener ESP cards, except that the symbols were the little horseshoes and cruces ansata of symbolic logic. He had ordered these cards on the Garaden Institute's money when he brought Belphebe from Faerie into his own continuum, and they were ready on his return from the *Orlando Furioso*. They ought to make the task of leaping from one universe to another considerably easier than by drawing the symbols on blank cards or sheets of paper. Beside him lay a copy of the *Kalevala*, to which he referred from time to time as he tried to sort out the logical premises of the continuum for proper arrangement of the cards.

' 'Lo, sweetheart,' he said abstractedly, as she came in with the big bundle, 'I think I've got this thing selective enough to drop us right into Vainamoinen's front yard.'

'Harold!'

'Huh?'

'The slot-hounds are surely on the trail. Two men in a police car sought to follow me on my way home.'

'Oh-oh. What happened?'

'I spun sprackly wise about a few corners and so eluded them for the time, but . . .'

'Oh, boy. They'll have your licence number and be here any time.'

'A pox and a murrain on them! What is there more to assemble? I'll have all ready in half an hour's space.'

'Not half an hour. Now. Stay there! No, don't try to put on those new clothes now. Hug the bundle and it'll come along with us. Get your bow and stuff.'

He jumped up and ran up the stairs. Presently his voice came, muffled from the depths of a closet. 'Belphebe!'

'Yes?'

'Where the hell are those thick wool socks of mine?'

'In the big carton. You haven't used them since last winter.'

'Okay . . . And that yellow scarf? Never mind, I found it . . .'

Minutes later, he reappeared in the living room with his arms full of clothing and equipment. To Belphebe he said, 'Got your bow? Good. And plenty of arr – '

The front doorbell rang.

Belphebe took a quick look out the window. ' 'Tis they! There squats their car! What's to do?'

'Beat it for the *Kalevala*, quick. Sit on the rug beside me and hold my hand with one hand and your duffel with the other.'

The bell rang again. Shea, throwing himself into the lotus posture of Yoga, concentrated on the cards in front of him.

'If A is not not-B, and B is not not-A . . .'

The room went out of focus.

There was nothing in front of him save the cards,

arranged in a square of five cards on a side. Twenty-five cards.

'. . . and if C be the Land of Heroes, the *Kalevala* . . .'

On went the spell. The cards dissolved into a million little spots of light, whirling in a rigadoon of their own mysterious meaning. Shea tightened his grip on Belphebe's hand and his bundle of gear.

There was a sensation of being borne, featherlight, along the avenues of a gale. Colours. Sounds that could not quite be heard. A feeling of falling. Shea remembered how he had been scared witless the first time this happened to him – and how at the end of it he had landed in Norse myth at the Ragnarok instead of the Irish myth he had desired . . .

The whirling lights sorted themselves out into a fixed pattern, solidfied, materialized. He was sitting in long, worn grass, with Belphebe and a couple of piles of clothes beside him.

Two

The grasses, nodding to a gentle breeze, closed in the view around them. Overhead a blanket of close-packed low clouds marched across Shea's vision, shutting off the sky. The air was mildly cool and moist. At least they had not arrived in the midst of one of those terrifying Finnish winters.

Shea gathered his long legs under him and rose with a grunt, pulling Belphebe up after him. Now he could see that they stood in a wide meadow. To their right, the meadow ran out into the edge of a forest of mixed birch and fir. To their left . . .

'Hey, kid! Look at those,' said Shea.

'Those' were a group of animals grazing around a big old oak that stood alone in the meadow. Shea made out three horses, rather small and shaggy, and another animal, belonging to the deer family. With antlers. Either a caribou or a very large reindeer.

'We shall not lack for meat,' said Belphebe. 'Certainly this is a noble stag, and too proud to fear.'

The four animals, after a ruminant look at the time-continuum travellers, had returned to their grazing.

'It must be a reindeer,' said Shea. 'They use them for draught animals around here.'

'Like the gift-giving sprite called Santa Claus in your legends of Ohio?'

'Yeah. Let's get our junk over to that fence and put on our woods clothes. Damn, I forgot toothbrushes. And extra underwear . . .'

He thought of other items he'd forgotten in their haste to get away, such as grease for their boots. However, there were two of them, and they had his well-tempered epee and her longbow, not to mention his command of magic. By the use of these in such an environment, it should be possible to get whatever else was really necessary.

The fence was one of the wood-rail, Abraham Lincoln type. As they neared it, picking up their feet to force them through the long grass, the forest opened out a bit, and Shea glimpsed a group of low, long log houses, half hidden among the trees. A thin blue plume of smoke issued from a hole in the roof of one. There was a faint sound of voices.

'People,' said Shea.

'Grant they may be friendly,' said Belphebe, glancing towards the buildings as she inserted herself into an angle of fence and began to pull her dress over her head.

'Don't worry, kid,' said Shea. 'Vainamoinen's the best egg in the whole space-time continuum.'

He began to change to his woods clothes.

'Oh, Harold,' said Belphebe. 'We brought with us no scrip or other carrier wherein to transport our possessions, and I am loath to leave this good dress. It was the first you bought me, when we were in New York.'

'Fold it up, and I'll make a bag out of my shirt. Hello, company's coming!'

They hurriedly completed their change and were lacing their boots, when the man who had appeared from the direction of the houses reached the gate in the fence and came towards them.

He was a short man, of about Harold Shea's own age (in other words, on the naive side of thirty), with a snub nose, wide Mongoloid cheek bones, and a short, straggly black beard. His thumbs were thrust into a broad embroidered leather belt that gathered in a linen blouse-shirt which fell over a pair of baggy, woollen pants, which in turn were tucked into boots with hair on the outside. A cap of some high-grade fur sat precariously on one side of his head. He swaggered notably.

Shea buckled on the scabbarded epee and said: 'Good day, sir!' confident that his transition to this continuum had automatically changed his language to the local one.

The man cocked his head on one side and combed his

beard with his fingers, surveying them from head to foot. Finally he spoke.

'Oh, ye funny-looking strangers,
It is plain for all to witness,
Ye are from a foreign country!
Tell me of yourselves, O strangers;
Whence ye come from, what your station,
Who your forebears, what the purpose
Brings you to the land of heroes?'

Oh, no you don't, thought Shea. I've read the *Kalevala*, and I know that when you get the ancestry of a man you can clap all sorts of spells on him. Aloud he said courteously, 'I'm Harold Shea, and this is my wife, Belphebe. We come from Ohio.'

'Harolsjei? Pelviipi? Ouhaio?' said the man.
'Truth to tell, I do not know them.
From a distant land ye must be,
Farther than the realm of Hiisi,
Than the dreaded deeps of Mana.
Though ye come a long way hither,
Never shall ye lack for welcome,
So that beautiful Pelviipi
Ever smooths the path before you
By her smile so warmly radiant,
Warmly radiant as the sunbeam.'

'Thanks,' said Shea drily. 'And if it's all the same to you, I'd just as soon you spoke prose. My wife was bitten by a poet once, and it gave her an allergy that makes her uncomfortable when she hears more of it.'

The man glanced at Shea suspiciously and at Belphebe appreciatively. 'Hear me now, O Harolainen . . .' he began, but Belphebe, playing up nobly, made a face and a slight retching sound, so he checked, and lowering his voice, said, 'Is it not that in far Ouhaio you control your women?'

'No, they control us,' said Shea rapidly.

Belphebe frowned; the stranger smiled ingratiatingly. 'In our noble land of heroes early do we learn the manner of teaching women their places. Now will I make you the fairest of offers – we shall for one wife exchange the other, and fair Pelviipi shall be returned to you, made most obedient, and with a knowledge of poetry gained from the greatest singer in all Kalevala, all the land of heroes.'

'Huh?' said Shea. 'No, I don't think I'd care to go into a deal like that . . .' and as he caught the stocky man's frown '. . . at least until I know more about your country. Is Vainamoinen up there at the houses?'

The stranger had been leading them towards the gap in the fence. He said sullenly, 'Not there now nor ever will be.'

'Oh,' said Shea, thinking that he must somehow have made a positional error. 'Then whom does this establishment belong to?'

The man stopped, drew himself up, and with as much hauteur as a shorter man can give himself before a taller, said,

'Stranger, it is clear as water
You are new to Kalevala.
No one from the land of heroes
Could mistake great Kaulkomieli,
Oft as Saarelainen mentioned.
Surely have the fame and glory
Of the lively Lemminkainen
Wafted to your distant country!'

'Oh-oh,' said Shea. 'Pleased to meet you, Lemminkainen. Ye-es, your fame has come to Ohio.'

He shot a nervous glance at Belphebe. Not having read the *Kalevala*, she was in no position to appreciate exactly how serious the positional error was. Instead of reliable old Vainamoinen, they had made contact with the most unreliable character in the whole continuum: Lemminkainen, the reckless wizard and arrant lecher.

But trying to pull out now would only make things worse. Shea went on, 'You have no idea what a pleasure it is to meet a real hero.'

'You have met the greatest,' said Lemminkainen, modestly. 'Doubtless you have come to seek aid against a fire bird or sea dragon that is laying waste your country.'

'Not exactly,' said Shea, as they reached the gate. 'You see, it's like this: we have a couple of friends who got stranded in another world, and the magic of our own world isn't strong enough to bring them back. So we thought we'd come to a country where they had real magicians and find somebody with skill enough to manage the job.'

Lemminkainen's broad face assumed an expression of immense craftiness. 'What price shall be offered for this service thaumaturgic?'

Damn it, thought Shea, can't the man speak plain language? Aloud he said, 'What might you want, for instance?'

The stocky man shrugged. 'I, the mighty Lemminkainen, have few needs of anybody. Flocks and herds in plenty have I, fields of rye and barley, girls to kiss and serfs to serve me.'

Shea exchanged a glance with Belphebe. As he stood there, debating whether to mention his own technique in magic, Lemminkainen went on, 'Perhaps, if the beautiful Pelviipi . . .'

'Not on your life!' said Shea quickly.

Lemminkainen shrugged again and grinned. 'As you wish, O Harolainen. I have no desire to haggle – and in any case, I have my own wrongs to right. Curses on the Mistress of Pohjola, who refused to let me wed her daughter, and not only that, did not even invite me to her wedding with Ilmarinen the smith. I will slay these wretched people of the land of fog and darkness!'

He suddenly snatched off his cap, flung it on the ground and danced up and down in a paroxysm of rage. Shea tried to recall his *Kalevala*. There was something about a journey of revenge like that in it, and it had not turned out too well for Lemminkainen, as he recalled.

'Wait a minute,' he said, 'maybe we can make a deal at that. This Pohjola is a pretty tough nut. If you take the two of us along, we might be of a good deal of help in cracking it.'

Lemminkainen stopped his capering. 'Shall a hero of my stature fear the land of frost and midnight?' he asked. 'Tall you are, but lack the mighty thews of Kalevala's heroes. You might help if the battle were with children.'

'Now look here,' said Shea, 'I may not be built like a truck-horse, but I can do one or two things. With this.' He whipped out the epee.

At Shea's draw, Lemminkainen's hand flashed to the hilt of his own broadsword, but he refrained from producing it when it was evident that Shea had no immediate intention of attacking him. He looked at the epee.

'Certainly that is the oddest sword-blade ever seen in Kalevala,' he said. 'Do you use it as a toothpick or with thread to patch your breeches?'

Shea grinned in his turn. 'Feel that point.'

'It is sharp, but my wife Kylliki does my darning.'

'Still, it wouldn't do you any good if it poked into you, would it? All right, then. Want to see how I use it?'

Lemminkainen's short, broad blade came out.

'No, Harold,' said Belphebe, putting down her own bundle and beginning to string her bow.

'It's all right, kid. I've dealt with these cut men before. Remember the hillside near Castle Carena? Besides, this is just practice.'

'Do you wish to try at flatsides?'

'Exactly. Ready?'

Clang-dzing-zip! went the blades. Lemminkainen, pressing forward, was as good a swordsman with the edge as Shea had ever encountered. He swung forehand, backhand and overhand with bewildering speed, not seeming even to breathe hard. His theory seemed to be to get in close and hit as hard and as often as possible, and to hell with the consequences.

Shea, backing slowly, parried the vicious swings slantwise, wondering what would happen if one of them caught his thin blade at a square enough angle to snap it off. A crack like that could maim or kill a man, even though only the flat of the blade was used. Once Shea tried a riposte; Lemminkainen leaped backward with catlike agility.

Round and round went Shea, giving ground steadily, trying to save his own breath. Once his foot was not quite firm; a swing almost got him and he had to stagger back three steps, with Belphebe's 'Oh!' in his ears. But at last the whirlwind attack slackened. The epee slid out and scratched along Lemminkainen's forearm.

'You can tickle with that piece of straw,' admitted the hero. He swung again, not so accurately this time. Shea turned the blade aside and the epee darted forward to scratch Lemminkainen's shoulder.

'See,' said Shea. Lemminkainen growled, but a quick attack brought the point squarely against his midriff before he could even begin an attempt at a parry.

'Now what would happen if I pushed?' said Shea.

'Boastful stranger, that was but a chance occurrence.'

'Oh, yeah? Well, let's try it again, then.'

Dzing-zip-tick-clang went the blades. This time Lemminkainen, though not in the least winded, was frowning and overanxious. There were only a couple of exchanges before he was off balance and once more Shea put his point against the broad chest before him. He said, 'That, my friend, was no accident. Not twice in a row.'

Lemminkainen sheathed his blade and waved a contemptuous hand. 'Against an unarmoured foe your tricks might gain you a few minutes more of life. But the men of black Pohjola go to war in mail. Do you think that little skewer will do them damage?'

'I don't know what kind of armour they have, but it had better be tight at the joints if they're going to keep this point out.'

'I will take you to Pohjola – but enough has not been

shown me that I should put the service of my magic to your need. You may be my servant.'

Shea shot a glance at Belphebe, who spoke up. 'Sir Lemminkainen, the men of your land are marvellous boasters, it appears, though falling somewhat short of the fulfilment of their claims. Yet if losing a contest makes one a servant, you shall be mine, for it would greatly astony me could you or any of yours surpass me in archery.'

Shea suppressed a grin. Belphebe might not have any formal training in psychology, but she knew how to deal with braggarts. The trick was to out-brag them on some point where you knew you could deliver the goods.

Lemminkainen squinted at Belphebe and said, 'Harolsjei, I withdraw my offer. In this wife of yours I see she is a vixen who needs nothing but chastisement. Wait for my returning.'

They were close to the buildings now. Shea noticed for the first time a row of ill-clad serfs who had been watching the contest with their mouths gaping open. 'My bow!' shouted Lemminkainen as they fell back before him.

Presently he was back with a crossbow under his arm and a fistful of bolts stuck in his belt. Shea noticed that the instrument had a bow of steel, with a strip of copper for backing and silver inlay. Quite a handsome piece of artillery, in fact.

'Harold,' said Belphebe, softly, 'not so certain am I that I can in truth best this knave. A strong crossbow of steel in practised hands can prove most deadly sure.'

'Do your best, kid, you'll slaughter him,' said Shea, feeling a good deal less confident than he sounded.

Lemminkainen said, 'Will you have a fixed mark, red-haired baggage, or shall I set a serf to run that we may have the better sport?'

'A fixed mark will do,' said Belphebe. She looked as though the only moving target she wanted was Lemminkainen.

The hero waved a hand. 'See that knot in yonder fence-post, distant from us forty paces?'

'I see it. 'Twill do as well as another.'

Lemminkainen grinned, cocked his bow and let drive. The steel-tipped bolt struck the fence-post with a loud crack, three or four inches below the knot.

Belphebe nocked an arrow, drew the string back to her ear, sighted a second and let go. The shaft grazed the edge of the fence-post and whistled off into the long grass.

Lemminkainen's grin widened. 'Another, would you?' This time he did even better; his bolt struck the post squarely, about an inch above the knot-hole. But Belphebe's shot stood quivering about the same distance below.

Lemminkainen shot another bolt, then shouted: 'I will not be outdone on this turn.' He seemed to be right; his quarrel was squarely in the knot.

A little frown appeared between Belphebe's eyes. She drew, held her draw for a couple of seconds, then lowered the bow and brought it up again to the release point in a single motion. The arrow struck the knot, right beside the bolt.

Shea said, 'Seems to me you're both about as good as you can get . . . Hey, why not try that?'

He pointed to where a big crow had flung itself on flapping wings out across the meadow, emitting a harsh *haw!*

Lemminkainen whipped up his crossbow and shot. The bolt whizzed upward, seeming to go right through the bird. A couple of black feathers drifted down, but after staggering in its flight, the crow kept on.

As the crow steadied, one of Belphebe's arrows sang upward and struck it with a meaty thump. It started to tumble; three more arrows streaked towards it in rapid succession. One missed, but two hit, so that the bird plummeted to earth with three arrows criss-crossing in its carcass.

Lemminkainen stared open-mouthed. There were murmurs from the serfs around the buildings. Belphebe said calmly, 'Now, sirrah, I should like my arrows back.'

Lemminkainen swung an arm to indicate that the serfs

should take up the task. Then he brightened, and tapped his own chest. 'I, the lively Lemminkainen, am still the greater hero,' he said, 'because I have excelled in two contests and each of you only in one. But it is not to be denied that you are very good persons of your hands, and in exchange for your help I will chant for you the magic runes you wish.'

Three

Two women appeared at the door of the main house as they approached in a little procession, with serfs now carrying the bundles. One of the women was old and wrinkled, the other young and rather buxom. It occurred to Shea that with a little makeup and a Mainbocher dress, she would be a very nice dish indeed. Lemminkainen seemed to be a good picker.

He said, 'Get you to the kitchen, women. We will have food, quickly, for it never shall be said that the great Kaukomieli is less than the most generous of hosts.'

As the pair started to turn away, Belphebe stepped forward and extended her hand to the older one. 'Gracious dame,' she said, 'forgive Sir Lemminkainen's seeming want of courtesy in not making us known to each other. He has no doubt been too much concerned with high matters. I am Belphebe of Faerie, wife to Sir Harold Shea here.'

The old woman grabbed Belphebe's hand. Her eyes filled with tears, and she murmured something unintelligible; then she turned and toddled rapidly into the depths of the house. The nice dish curtsied. 'I am known as Kylliki, the maid of Saari, wife of Lemminkainen,' she said, 'and she there is his mother. You are welcome.'

Lemminkainen regarded her sourly. 'Women always must be gabbling,' he said. 'Come, guests from Ouhaiola, let yourselves sit down and tell me of this conjuring you wish. I need the names and stations of the persons you wish brought here; who were their forebears, where they now may be, all that is known of them. Moreover though your skill in magic may be small as compared with that of so accomplished a wizard as myself, it were well if you added your spells to mine; for it is by no means to be concealed that this is a very difficult task, to draw men from one world to another.'

Shea frowned. 'I can tell you a good deal about one of them. Dr Walter Simms Bayard, Ph.D. in psychology from Columbia University, class of – umm – nineteen-forty. He's from – mmm – born in Atlantic City, New Jersey, I believe. Father was – Oswald Bayard, a business-man. Had a department store in Atlantic City. Died a couple of years ago.'

Lemminkainen said, 'Strange and hard are the names you pronounce, O Harol! And the mother of this Payart? I must have the smallest details of his pedigree and background.'

Shea gave what little he knew about Bayard's mother, who lived in New York with another son of the family, and whom he, Shea, had met briefly.

Lemminkainen closed his eyes in an effort of memory, then asked, 'And the other whom you would draw to the land of heroes?'

Shea scratched his head. 'That's a tough one. All I know about him is that he's a detective of our police force, that his name is Pete and that he breathes through his mouth. Must have adenoids or something. A suspi-cious character and not too bright.'

Lemminkainen shook his head. 'Though it is well known that I am one of the greatest of all magicians, I can have no power over one so meagrely depicted as this.'

Belphebe spoke up. 'Why don't you try getting Walter here first by himself? Perchance in Xanadu, where he is now, he will have learned enough of this Pete to enable Lemminkainen to conjure him up.'

'Okay, kid, I think you've got it. Go ahead with Bayard, Lemminkainen, and we'll worry about Pete afterwards.'

Just at this moment the women came back from the kitchen with another wearing the crude clothes and deferential air of a serf, all three carrying big wooden plates. Each plate bore a huge hunk of rye-bread, a couple of pork chops and a wedge of cheese the size of Shea's fist. Another serf followed with huge mugs of beer.

Lemminkainen said, 'Eat as you will. This little snack

should edge your appetite for supper.'

Shea's eyes bugged. He said to Belphebe: 'I wonder what these people would call a real meal.'

Lemminkainen said, 'We must eat whole mounds of victuals to enhance our souls for such a journey.'

The old woman, his mother, gave a little cry. 'Do not go, my son. You are not proof against death.'

Lemminkainen spoke around a huge mouthful of food. 'No, it is now a thing decided. Little though a hero of my prowess needs the help of others, it is still true as the proverb has it, that bare is the back with no brother behind it, and these strangers of Ouhaiola may help me much.'

'But you promised me you would not go,' said Kylliki.

'That was before I met these strangers with the strange sword and the strange bow.'

The old woman began to cry, wiping her eyes with the hem of her dress. 'You are not wanted there. They will set traps of magic all across your way as soon as they know you are coming, and neither the strangers nor your own strength can keep you from death.'

Lemminkainen laughed, spraying the table with fragments of cheese. 'Fear is for the women only – and not all of those,' he said, and gave Belphebe an admiring glance. Shea began to wonder whether he had not been a little hasty in persuading this buck to accept their services. 'Now, go fetch me my finest shirt, for I will no longer delay in starting to show those snakes of Pohjola how we keep feast in the land of heroes.'

He stood up and walked around the table towards Kylliki with one hand drawn back. Shea wondered if the hero was going to hit her and wondered what he himself would do if Lemminkainen did, but the nice little dish saved him the trouble of doing anything by getting up hastily and scuttling out of the room. Lemminkainen came back, sat down, took a long drink of beer and wiped his mouth on the back of his hand.

'Let us to our spells, O Harol,' he said amiably. 'I must think a moment that the verses run smoothly.'

'So must I,' said Shea, producing pencil and a piece of paper from his pocket, and beginning to set up a sorites. He would have to allow for the fact that the poetic element in this Finnish magic was very strong indeed, and probably interminably long. Belphebe slid down towards the end of the bench where Lemminkainen's mother was sitting and began talking to her in a low tone. She seemed to be getting results, too, because the old lady was looking noticeably less woebegone.

After a few minutes Kylliki came back with a clean white shirt, and another of some kind of leather with fishscale metal plates sewed on to it in an overlapping pattern, which she laid on the bench beside Lemminkainen. The hero rewarded her by pulling her down beside him.

'Now you shall hear one of my greatest spells,' he said, 'for I have composed well and truly. Are you ready, Harol?'

'About as ready as I will be,' said Shea.

Lemminkainen leaned back, closed his eyes, and began to sing in a high tenor voice.

'O, thou distant Valter Payart,
Caught in Xanadu's enchantments,
I am sure I know thy father,
Since thy father's name was Osvalt . . .'

There didn't seem to be much of a tune, or rather each line had a tune of its own.

'Osvalt of Atlantic City,
And thy mother's name was Linda,
Of the New York City Jacksons,
See I know of all thy people . . .'

He droned on and on, while Shea tried to concentrate on the sorites. With the back of his mind he was forced to concede that the big lug was probably a pretty good magician. His memory was prodigious, for he hadn't left out a single item of the Bayard biography and connections, though he had heard them only once.

Lemminkainen's verses came faster and faster, until with his voice climbing the scale, he ended.

'Come thou now, O Valter Payart,
From the pleasure-dome of Kubla,
To the land of Kalevala.
Thou canst not resist my singing,
Canst not delay your coming;
Thou art standing here before us!'

Lemminkainen's voice rose to a scream on the last words; he stood up and swept both hands around his head in a series of magical passes.

Foomp!

There was a rush of displaced air, which rattled the wooden plates around the room, and there was Dr Walter Simms Bayard of the Garaden Institute, Ph.D. in psychology.

Not, however, standing before them. He was sitting cross-legged on the floor, and lying on her back across his lap, clinched in a passionate kiss with him, was one of the houris of Xanadu, wearing about as much as a burlesque queen at the climax of her performance.

Bayard removed his mouth from that of the girl to look around him with amazed eyes.

Lemminkainen said, 'Now is it to be seen that I am truly the greatest of wizards. For not only have I conjured this man from another world, but his handmaiden also. O Valtarpayart, fitting it is that you should give her to me in reward for my services.'

As Bayard released her and both of them began to scramble up, Belphebe plucked at Shea's arm.

'Look at Kylliki,' she said in a low voice. 'She looks as though she wanted to scratch somebody's eyes out.'

'She'll get over it,' said Shea. 'Besides, if I know Walter, he isn't going to fall for Lemminkainen's bright ideas any more than I did.'

'That's what I mean. Harold.' Her voice became still lower. 'Isn't it true that in this continuum if you know everything about a person, you can always put some kind of spell on them?'

'Gee, you're right, kid. I never thought about it. We'll have to keep an eye on Walter.'

Four

Bayard's face slowly turned the colour of a well-ripened strawberry. 'Look here, Harold,' he said, 'these tricks of yours . . .'

'I know,' said Shea, 'you were just getting acclimated.' Belphebe giggled and Lemminkainen guffawed. 'Skip it – we haven't got time for temperament. This is Lemminkainen. He's a hero with a capital H.'

'How do you do,' said Bayard, a trifle loftily, and held out his hand. The hefty man, grinning all over his face at the complimentary description, did not appear to notice it, but ducked a kind of bow from where he sat on the bench. It occurred to Shea that the custom of handshaking probably hadn't been introduced in this continuum.

The thought apparently did not occur to Bayard. He frowned darkly, placed a protecting arm around his houri's shoulders, and said, 'This is Miss Dunyazad – Mrs Shea, Mr Harold Shea. Now, Harold, if you'll tell me how to get out of this Norse madhouse, I'll get about it. I don't blame you for bringing me here, of course, but I haven't your taste for adventure.'

'It isn't Norse, it's Finnish,' said Shea. He grinned. 'And I don't think you're going to get out right away. I don't think it would look good if you turned up at the Garaden Institute with your Miss Dunyazad and without Pete the cop. At least Belphebe and I found it that way. By the way, I hope he didn't get himself impaled or anything?'

Bayard looked a little mollified as the houri snuggled closer to him. 'Oh, he's making the best of a bad business, trying to beat off the Rockette chorus. He's really a very proper Presbyterian, a deacon of the church. The last thing I heard him doing was trying to teach one of the girls the doctrine of original sin. By the way, is there anything solid to eat around here? I'm fed up to the ears with that sticky mess they gave us in Xanadu.'

Lemminkainen had been engaged in a huge yawn that showed his tonsils and a great deal else. Now he brought his mouth closed with a snap. 'True it is, O noble guestlings, that in the fatigue of my mighty magic, I forget the first duty of a host. Kylliki! Mother! Fetch supper.' He counted guests on his fingers. 'A couple of dozen ducks will do. Valtarpayart, I see your handmaiden is dressed for the bath. Does she wish one prepared?'

'No,' said Bayard, 'but I think she could use the loan of some clothes if you have a few to spare. Couldn't you, my dear?'

Dunyazad nodded dumbly and, as Lemminkainen shouted for clothes, Bayard led her over to a bench and sat down. Shea noticed it was as far as possible from Lemminkainen.

Bayard said, 'I don't wish to cavil, Harold, but I really don't see why it was necessary to involve me in this escapade of yours.'

Shea explained the magical reasons for the flank attack on Xanadu. 'But we still haven't got Pete the cop, and if we ever want to get back to Ohio, we'd better. How much do you know about him? Irish, isn't he?'

'I should say not! I talked with him enough to find out that in spite of being a Presbyterian, his real name is Brodsky, and he's about as Irish as Jawarharlal Nehru. He only wishes he were Irish, tells Irish jokes and sings Irish songs. With that polyp or something he has in his nose, the result is below Metropolitan Opera standards.'

Kylliki came through the door, bringing with her an odour of cooking duck and a long, loose dress which she threw at rather than handed to Dunyazad. Lemminkainen's eyes followed the houri admiringly as she struggled into it. Then he yawned again and said, 'Scanty is the tale you give me of this Piit whom you are seeking.'

'Well,' said Bayard, 'let's see. He was promoted to second grade detective for the work he did on the Dupont case. I've heard that a dozen times. He works out of the

Madison Street station. His mother is named Maria, and his father was named Pete, too, and was a bricklayer, and wanted him to tend bar when he grew up. He himself had the idea of being a pro football player. Will that do?'

Lemminkainen shook his head gloomily. 'Only such a master of magic as I would dare attempt the passing-spell with materials so scanty. And even I must meditate on it until morning, for I am foredone with labours mighty.'

'Why not now?' Bayard appealed to Shea. 'I'd like to see how this is done. I may be able to use it,'

Shea shook his head. 'Won't do, honest, Walter. You don't know the first thing about magic yet. It has rational rules, but they follow a different kind of logic from anything you've had any experience with. And I wouldn't advise you to stay around while Lemminkainen is fishing for Pete, either. You've worked up quite a bit of magical potential by being pulled here from Xanadu. So if Lemminkainen does fetch Pete, and you're right here handy, you're a little bit apt to pop right back into Xanadu along the lines of weakness created by the spell while he's coming here. Remember the trouble we had, dear?'

'Marry, that do I,' said Belphebe. 'But let us not dwell upon it, for here's our sup.'

This time there were seven servants in the procession. Each bore a wooden tray upon which a mountain of bread was surrounded by three whole roast ducks except the one who served Lemminkainen. He had six.

When he had finished the last of them, with one of the ducks Shea was unable to eat, he stretched, yawned again, and said, 'Harol, friend and helper of the lively Lemminkainen, you shall have tonight the lock bed. Will you lead Pelviipi to it? As for these guests, the late-comers, they shall have my best of bearskins to compose them by the hearth-fire. Come, Kylliki, lead me bedward, for I cannot walk unaided.'

Shea thought the spell must have taken a lot out of the big oaf at that as he watched him stagger towards his sleeping quarters, but had to admit that Limmenkainen was cheerfully keeping to his side of their bargain, even if he did talk in that phony poetry.

One of the servants with a rush torch showed him and Belphebe down to the end of the hall where the lock bed was. It was bigger than a Pullman section, but not very much, and both of them had to roll up clothes for pillows . . .

'What the hell's that?' said Shea, sitting upright and cocking an ear towards the foot of the bed.

Belphebe giggled where she lay. 'That, my most puissant and delectable lord, would seem to be the hero and his spouse engaged in a sport we wot of – to wit, a quarrel within the household. Hark! She has just called him frog spawn.'

Shea gazed at the partition which separated them from the room to which Lemminkainen had retired. 'Well, I hope they get over it soon,' he said. 'With your woods-trained ears, you can make out what they're saying and enjoy the show, but all it sounds like to me is a racket.'

They did get through with it fairly soon, at that. But now the reindeer skins that served as blankets were too hot when they were on and he was too cold with them off. Besides, the straw mattress resembled a relief map of the Himalayas, and he never could get used to sleeping in a place where there weren't any windows, even if cracks in the outer wall did admit enough air.

Something scratched at the door of the lock bed.

Shea listened for a minute, then turned over.

The something scratched again, this time in what was clearly a signal, for the scratching came one – two – three.

Shea jackknifed to a sitting posture in the Pullman berth and slid the door of the lock bed open a crack. Down the hall, the fire on the hearth was at the ember stage, throwing a red light over the two mounds beside it that must be Bayard and his Dunyazad. It gave just illumination enough for Shea to make out the figure of the nice little dish, Kylliki, bending over at the entrance to the lock bed. One finger went to her lips and then beckoned.

Shea experienced a dreadful if momentary sinking of the heart at the thought he might have a female wolf on his hands, but Kylliki settled the question for him by sliding the door of the lock bed farther open and reaching past him to touch Belphebe into wakefulness, then sat down on the edge of the lock bed. When the couple had taken their places beside her, she leaned close and said in a stage whisper. 'There is treason afoot.'

'Oh-oh,' said Shea. 'What kind?'

'My husband, the hero Kaukomieli. Who can resist him?'

'I dunno, but we can give it the old college try. What's he up to?'

'I learned but now his purpose. 'Tis to evade the making of the spell for bringing from hence to hither your other friend. Such wizardries leave him always weak and foredone, as you saw but this evening.'

'Why, the . . .' began Shea, reaching for his epee, but Belphebe said, 'Hold, Harold, there must be more in this than meets the eye, and meseems it's more a matter for craft than violence,' She turned to Kylliki. 'Why do you give us this tale? It cannot be a matter of concern for you whether this Pete be summoned or no.'

In the darkness they could plainly hear the girl grind her teeth. 'Because of the other wing to his bird of thought,' she flared. 'Instead of going to Pohjola, he'd be off to the lakes with that immodest she-devil who wears no clothes.'

'Dunyazad. What do you want us to do about it?'

'Be off,' said Kylliki. 'Take him to Pohjola with the dawn. It is the lesser peril.'

Shea thought of Lemminkainen's barrel-like chest and huge arms. 'I don't see how we're going to make him do anything he doesn't want to,' he said.

Kylliki laid a hand on his arm. 'You do not know my lord. This night he lies weaker than a newborn reindeer calf with the back-whip of his spell-making. I have a rope.

Bind him while the weakness is on him, and steal him away.'

Belphebe said, 'I think she has the key that will unlock our troubles, Harold. If we bind Lemminkainen tonight, then we can keep him tied up until he makes the spell that will bring Pete. And then he will be too weary to think on revenges.'

'Good for you, kid,' said Shea, heaving himself to his feet and reaching for his pants. 'All right, let's go. But I think we'll need Walter to help.'

Getting Walter was not so easy as it looked. He was sleeping the sleep of the just after his prolonged vacation in Xanadu, and shaking him only produced a series of contented grunts. Dunyazad's head came out of the bearskins though, to look at the three standing over her with mild, cow-like eyes, not saying a word, even when Kylliki hissed at her like a cat. Shea decided that Dunyazad belonged to the beautiful-but-dumb type.

After an interminable time, Bayard pulled himself together and accompanied Shea into Lemminkainen's room, where a rush-light held by Kylliki showed the hero sprawled cornerwise across the bed with all his clothes on, fully dressed and snoring like a sawmill. He didn't even move when Shea cautiously lifted a leg to put a coil of rawhide rope around it, and only changed the rhythm of his snores as they rolled him back and forth, wrapping him like a cocoon in the tough rawhide.

Kylliki said, 'His mother will think little good of this, the old harridan! She cares for nothing save that he stays by her hand. I could tear her hair out.'

'Why don't you?' suggested Shea, with a yawn. 'Well, come on, kid, let's try to get a little shut-eye. When that big lug comes to, it will be like trying to sleep in the same house as a steam calliope.'

He was amply borne out after what seemed little more than ten minutes of slumber, and jerked out of bed to follow Bayard into the other room, from which a series of truly majestic howls were emerging.

Lemminkainen was rolling around the floor of the room shrieking curses and trying to writhe loose, while Kylliki, with no attempt at all to disguise the sneer on her pretty face, was cursing just as fast at him. Suddenly, the hero relaxed, screwed up his face, and in his singing voice began to chant:

'Think you that I'll heed your wishes,
Now you've flouted and provoked me,
By your strategems and insults?
I will live to see you, strangers,
All except the fair Tunjasat,
Hurled into the depths of Mana,
Down to Hiisi's kingdom tumbling!
Think you that this rope can hold me,
Me, the wizard Kaukolainen?
Just observe how from my members
Are the cords impotent falling!'

Shea stared; it was true. The cords around his feet were working loose. He tried to think of a counter-spell.

Bayard said, 'Hey, cut that out!' He seemed to be addressing a point a foot or two beyond Lemminkainen.

'Cut what out?' asked Shea.

'Untying him.'

'But if his magic . . .'

'Magic my foot! I'm talking about the old lady.'

'What old lady?' said Shea.

'I guess she's Lemminkainen's mother. Are you blind?'

'Apparently I am. You mean she's there, invisible, untying him?'

'Certainly, but she's not in the least invisible.'

The coils of rope had worked themselves loose from feet, ankles and knees. The triumphantly grinning Lemminkainen gave a massive wriggle and came to his feet.

'Well, for Lord's sake, stop her!' said Shea.

'Huh? Oh, yes, I suppose so.' Bayard stepped over to where Lemminkainen was standing and grabbed at the air. There was a scream; a couple of feet away from the hero, Lemminkainen's mother materialized with her hair over her eyes, glaring as Bayard held both her hands. Kylliki glared right back at her.

'Now, now,' said Shea. 'We're not going to hurt your son, lady. Only make sure that he carries out his part of the bargain.'

'An evil bargain. You will take him to his death,' croaked the old woman.

'And you would make him a woman-bound weakling instead of a hero,' snapped Kylliki.

'That's right,' said Shea. 'Must say I'm disappointed in you, Kauko.'

A portentous frown had replaced Lemminkainen's smile. 'How mean you?' he demanded.

'Here I thought you were the greatest hero of Kalevala, and you get cold feet over the Pohjola project.'

Lemminkainen gave an inarticulate bellow, then subsided to a mere roar. 'Me, afraid? By Jumala, loose me from these bonds and I'll make you a head shorter to show you how afraid I am!'

'Nothing doing, Toots. You fetch Pete from Xanadu, and then we'll discuss any changes of plan.'

The hero put on his crafty expression. 'If your friend the spry detective is brought here from Xanadu, will you, Payart, give me the fair Tunjasat?'

'I really don't think . . .' began Bayard, but Shea cut him off with, 'Nothing doing. That wasn't in the original contract. You go right ahead, or the whole deal's off.'

'Well, then. But from these bonds you must release me, else my magic spells will falter.'

Shea swung to Kylliki. 'Can I trust him?' he asked.

Her head came up, 'Fool! My husband is no promise-breaker . . . But – he may put a spell on Payart to make him yield up the maiden.'

Shea stepped across to Lemminkainen and began to untie knots. 'That's right, Walter. And besides, there's the danger that you might get blown back into Xanadu by the spell. You bettter get out of here, as far away from the building as you can. I don't know what the local range of magic is, but it can't be very high.'

Bayard made for the door. As the last loop fell from his arms, Lemminkainen stretched them over his head, sat down and corrugated his forehead in thought. At last he said, 'Are you ready, Harold? Good – let us begin.'

He tilted back his head and sang.

'Oh, I know thee, Peter Protsky,
And from Xanadu I call thee . . .'

He droned on. Shea quietly worked away on the sorites. Up and up went the voice of Lemminkainen, and just as it almost reached screaming pitch, in through the door came Dunyazad, her lovely, vacant face inquiring.

'Have you seen my lord?' she asked.

'. . . thou art with us!' finished Lemminkainen, on a high C.

There was a rush of air; for a moment only a cloud of burning sparks hung where the houri had been, and then they went out, leaving the space occupied by a solid-looking man in a rumpled brown American business suit.

Five

'What the hell is this?' Pete said, and then his eye fell on Harold Shea. 'Shea! You're under arrest! Kidnapping and resisting an officer!'

Shea said, 'I thought we'd been all through that.'

'Oh, you did, did you? And you thought you could stash me away in that screwball fairyland while you went on and rolled your hoop? Well, you've got staging an indecent theatrical performance on top of the other charges now. How do you like that? You better come along with me.'

'Come along where?' said Shea.

'Huh?' Pete Brodsky looked around the room and at the slumping Lemminkainen. 'Bejabbers, where is this dump?'

'In Kalevala.'

'And where would that be? Canada?'

Shea explained. 'And here's the wife I'm supposed to have kidnapped or murdered. Darling, this is Detective Brodsky. Pete, this is Belphebe. Does she look dead?'

'Are you really the dame that disappeared at that picnic, back in Ohio?' asked Brodsky.

'Marry, that I am,' said Belphebe, 'and through no fault of my husband's either.'

'And in the second place,' said Shea, 'you're out of your bailiwick. You haven't any authority here.'

'You con-merchants always try to play it smart, don't you? The law of close pursuit takes care of that. Constructively, I've been in close pursuit of you ever since you pulled that last one on me back in Ohio. Where's the nearest American consul?'

'Better ask Lemminkainen. He's the local boss.'

'The big guy? Can he speak English?'

Shea smiled. 'You got along all right in Xanadu, didn't

you? You're speaking Finnish without knowing it.'

'Okay. Say, mister . . .'

Lemminkainen had been sitting slumped over. Now he lifted his head. 'Get you hence and let me sorrow,' he said. 'Ah, that by my own efforts I should be deprived of the embraces of the beautiful Tunjasat!' He glared at Shea. 'Man of ill-omen,' he said, 'if I but had my strength, there would be an accounting.'

Kylliki said, 'Much strength will come to him who eats good food.'

Lemminkainen appeared to brighten at the thought. 'Then why do you waste time in foolish chatter when food is lacking?' he said practically, and Kylliki scuttled out, followed by his mother.

Shea went off to hunt up Bayard and explain what had happened to Dunyazad. The psychologist did not seem unbearably grieved. 'An excellent exercise for the libido,' he said. 'but I fear that in time she would have become importunate. Persons of her order of intelligence frequently consider that beauty entitles them to great consideration without effort.' He accompanied Shea back into the house for breakfast.

Lemminkainen took his in his bedroom while the other three ate with Pete Brodsky, who did prodigious execution to a breakfast of roast meat, cheese and beer, belching appreciatively afterwards.

'Maybe I got you Joes kinda wrong.' he said, as he wiped his mouth with a dirty handkerchief. 'You may be all right guys at that – sorta elect, if you get me. Gimme the pitch, will you?'

Shea told him as well as possible what had happened in the continuum of Ariosto's *Orlando Furioso* and why Vaclav Polacek and Dr Reed Chalmers were still there. 'But,' he continued virtuously, 'we couldn't very well leave you and Walter Bayard in Xanadu, could we?'

'I get it,' said Brodsky. 'You figured you had to spring us out of that reefer-dream or else pull a bit yourself. Okay, so you're a square. What's the next lay?'

Shea told him about the Pohjola project. Brodsky

looked glum. 'So we gotta go up there and crack this box with a lot of them doorshakers on the lay? Me, I don't like it. Why can't we just take it on the lam for Ohio? I'll kill the rap for you.'

Shea shook his head. 'Not me. Especially after the fuss I made about Lemminkainen running out on his end of the bargain. Listen, you're in a place where magic works, and it's funny stuff. When you get something by promising something else, and then try not to deliver, you're apt to find yourself without the thing you wanted.'

'You mean if we went lamester, this Bayard and me would land back in that de luxe hoppen?'

'Something like that.'

Brodsky shook his head. 'You're shot with horseshoes that you got a Joe with you that believes in predestination. Okay, when do we take it?'

'Probably tomorrow. Lemminkainen knocked himself out bringing you from Xanadu and won't be fit till then.'

'I got it,' said Brodsky. 'What we got for today? Just bending the ears?'

Shea turned around and looked out the window. 'I guess so,' he said. 'It seems to have started raining.'

It was a long day. Kylliki and Lemminkainen's mother trotted in and out, carrying trays of food to the recumbent hero, and occasionally dropping one off at the table in the hall, where Brodsky and Walter Bayard had started an endless discourse on predestination, original sin, and Cartesianism. After a while, Shea and Belphebe wandered off into a corner and let them talk, since neither Kylliki nor the mother seemed very sociable. It had already grown towards evening and the lowering skies were definitely darker, though none of the rush-lights had been kindled, when Bayard and Brodsky approached the couple.

'Say, listen,' said the detective. 'Me and this Bayard, we been thinking, and we worked up a hot lineup. You know this magic stuff. How about you putting one of these spells on Lemon Meringue there, and make him drop his score on this Pohjola joint – just skip it? Then he just springs us back where we belong, see?'

Shea was doubtful. 'I don't know. There's likely to be a kick-back. He's a pretty hot wizard, and playing on his home grounds, where he knows all the rules and I don't. Besides, I warned you about what happens when you try to get out of a magical bargain.'

'But look here,' said Bayard, 'we aren't proposing anything unethical, even in the terms of magic. All we're suggesting is a spell that will make him see things our way. He'll have the credit of having performed a great action in rescuing us, which these heroes of romance prize more highly than anything else, as I gather it. As a more material reward, you can leave him some of your artifacts. That sword of yours, or Belphebe's bow, for instance.'

Shea turned to his wife. 'What do you say, kid?'

'I like it none too well, but I can see no true argument contrarious. Do as you will, Harold.'

'Well, I suppose doing almost anything's better than doing nothing.' He stood up. 'Okay, I'll try.'

He managed to waylay Lemminkainen's mother to ask her something about the hero's background, bearing in mind that one of the requirements of Kalevala magic was a fairly intimate acquaintance with the person or thing you were going to put a spell on. It was like putting soap in a geyser; the old dame prattled away at a furious pace, and Shea soon discovered that his own memory was by no means the equal of Lemminkainen's, so that he had to re-open the floodgates a couple of times by asking her to repeat.

The process lasted through another of the gigantic Kalevalan meals; when it was over Shea retired to the corner of the fireplace with a big mug of beer and tried to work out a chant in iambic tetrameters along the line Lemminkainen had used. The form wasn't very familiar to him and he kept forgetting lines, so he got a charred stick and tried scratching some of the key-words on the floor. While he was about it, the others drifted off to bed. Bayard was already snoring from his pile of bearskins when Shea, satisfied at last, took one of the rushlights, made his way to the door of the hero's bedroom, and in a low voice, chanted his composition.

As he finished, something seemed to flash before his eyes and he felt a little dizzy. It might be the beer, but he rather thought the spell had worked, and he staggered weakly across to the lock bed, almost missing the bracket when he put the rush-light in it.

Belphebe sat up, with the skin-blankets gathered close around her chin; her expression was far from welcoming.

' 'Lo, sweetheart,' said Shea. He hiccupped slightly, sat down on the bed and started to take off his boots.

Belphebe said, 'Begone, sir. I'm an honest wife.'

'Huh?' said Shea. 'Who ever said you were anything else? And why the fire-alarm?'

He reached out an arm for her. Belphebe wriggled towards the back of the bed, her voice suddenly going high. 'Harold! Walter! Help – I am beset!'

Shea looked at her in bewilderment. Why was she dodging him? He hadn't done anything. And why was she calling for 'Harold' when he was right there?

Before he could think up anything intelligent to say, Bayard's voice said from behind him, 'He's in it again – grab him and tie him up till Harold can do something about it.'

'Is everybody crazy?' demanded Shea, and felt Brodsky grab his arm. He pulled loose and threw a punch at the detective, which the latter dodged with a slight movement of his head. Then the light went out.

Shea awakened with a splitting headache and a dark brown taste in his mouth. There had been too much beer; and on top of that he was hogtied even more efficiently than he had bound Lemminkainen the previous night. It was just about dawn; somewhere outside he could hear a clink of metal as a serf went about the early business of the house. The two piles of bearskins near him on the floor would be Bayard and Brodsky.

'Hey, you guys!' he called. 'What happened?'

One set of snores bit off, a head lifted and Brodsky's

voice said, 'Listen, glom. We dropped you dead bang. Now dummy up before I let you have it again.'

Shea fumed inwardly, From the feeling at the side of his cranium Brodsky had let him have it all right, and with a peculiarly solid blackjack. The prospect of another treatment had no appeal. But he could not understand why everybody was behaving that way – unless perhaps Lemminkainen had put some kind of spell on him while he was trying to work on the hero. That must be it, Shea decided, and lay uncomfortably, trying to work out a counter-spell in Kalevalan terms. While he was doing that he must have drifted off into a doze again. He wakened to a roar of laughter.

It was fully light. The entire household was standing around him, including Belphebe with a worried expression, and the laughter came from Lemminkainen, who was doubled up, choking with mirth. Bayard merely looked surprised.

The master of the house finally got his breath long enough to say: 'Fetch me a pail of water, Kylliki – ho, ho, ho! – and we'll give his proper semblance to this son of Ouhaiola.'

Kylliki brought the pail. Lemminkainen crooned a spell over it, then dashed it into Shea's face.

'Harold!' cried Belphebe. She threw herself down on Shea and covered his wet and sputtering face with kisses. 'You left me burning anxious when you came not to me last night. I had thought you taken in some trap.'

'Help me off with this rope,' said Shea. 'What do you mean I didn't come to you? How do you think I got in this jam?'

'Nay, I see it now,' said the girl. 'You put on the appearance of Lemminkainen. Was it to test me?'

'Yeah,' said Brodsky. 'Sorry I sapped you, Shea, but how the hell was we to know?'

Shea stretched cramped arms and scratched a stubbly chin. He had put a line about 'As if we were twins identic' into his spell the previous night, and it appeared now that this had been a mistake. 'I was trying a little spell,' he said, 'and I guess it must have backfired.'

'You were twin to Lemminkainen,' said the hero. 'Learn, strange man from Ouhaiola, that the laws of magic tell us when a spell is falsely woven, all things wear another semblance. Nevermore seek to equal the master of magic until you know more of the art.' He turned. 'Mother! Kylliki! We must fall to eating, for we have a journey before us.'

Belphebe said to Shea. 'Harold, it is well to be warned. This saying that if a spell isn't accurate it will give another look to things is well to remember.'

'Yeah, the laws of magic are different here. But I wish we'd known that last night.'

They took their places at the table. Lemminkainen was in the best of humours, crowing over Shea's discomfiture and boasting of what he would do to the Pohjolans when he got to them. He seemed to have forgotten about Dunyazad or any other squab.

His mother looked more and more melancholy. At last she said, 'If you will not hear me for your own sake, at least listen for mine. Will you leave your mother alone and unprotected?'

'Little protection is needed,' said the hero. 'But such as you need, I give you. This Payart, this Piit shall stay with you. Not that the two together would be of one-third as much use as such a hero as myself.'

'Harold . . .' began Bayard, and Brodsky said, 'Hey, ain't we going with?'

Lemminkainen shook his head firmly. 'Never shall I consent. This is hero's work. Harolsjei has shown he can be a fighting man of sorts, and this shield-maiden is not the worst archer in the world, though far from so good as I am – but you, frogs of Ouhaio, what can you do?'

'Listen, lug,' said Brodsky, getting to his feet, 'come on outside, and I'll show you. I don't care if you're as big as Finn McCool.'

Bayard put out a restraining hand. 'Just a minute, Pete,' he said. 'I rather think he's right, at that. The kind of activity in which we are skilled is of little value in this continuum, and we might be more useful preserving the base, as it were.' He glanced at Kylliki. 'Besides, it occurs to me that perhaps you could improve the hour. I doubt if any of these people have heard of predestination and original sin.'

'Say, you're a good head,' said Brodsky, sitting down again. 'Maybe if we make that gift good, I could get a couple of converts.'

Lemminkainen was already on his feet, leading his way to the door. He took down a long rawhide lariat from a peg and headed out towards the meadow, where the same quartet of animals were grazing. They started walking away; the hero swung the rope and cast it over the nearest antler of an enormous reindeer. Then, chanting something about 'Elk of Hiisi', he climbed down the rope and made a loop around the animal's neck with the other end. The reindeer bucked; Lemminkainen gave one jerk and it went down on its knees.

Pete Brodsky's eyes opened wide. 'Lord!' he said softly, 'maybe I copped the right dope not trying to go on the muscle with that ghee.'

Lemminkainen started back across the meadow, leading the reindeer as though it were a puppy. Suddenly he stopped and stiffened. Shea followed his glance and saw that a man, too well dressed for a serf, was standing at the door of the main house, talking to Kylliki. As they came closer, it was apparent that the man was about Lemminkainen's own height, but stouter, with a great grey Santa Claus beard. He turned a beaming smile on the hero; they fell into each other's arms and administered powerful slaps on their respective backs, then held each other at arm's length. The stranger declaimed,

'Hail, the lively Lemminkainen!
Is it true thou plan'st to visit
In the fogbound land of Turja,
And with help of foreign swordsmen
Teach old Ilpotar a lesson?'

They fell into each other's arms and slapped again. 'Will you go with me to Pohjola?' bawled Lemminkainen.

'Nay, I still seek a new wife!' shouted the grey-bread, and both of them laughed as though this were a peculiarly brilliant jest.

Brodsky and Bayard pressed close to Shea and muttered questions. Shea said, 'The old guy must be Vainamoinen, the great minstrel and magician. Damn, if I'd known where to find him, I wouldn't have made that deal . . .'

'What old guy?' asked Bayard.

'The one talking to Lemminkainen and whacking him on the back. The one with the beard.'

'I don't see any such person,' said Bayard. 'He's hardly more than an adolescent, with only the beginnings of whiskers.'

'What!'

'Not over twenty.'

Shea exclaimed, 'Then this must be another magical illusion, and he must be after something. Watch him!'

The pseudo-Vainamoinen seemed to be trying to question Lemminkainen, but every now and then one of them would get off five or six lines of poetry, they would fall into each other's arms and begin back-slapping again. Suddenly, at the beginning of one of these declamations, Brodsky leaped, catching the stranger's wrist just as it came sweeping down. The detective twisted deftly, pulled the wrist across his own shoulders and stooped forward. The man's feet flew up, he came down on his head in the long grass with a wicked-looking knife in his hand. Brodsky deliberately kicked him in the ribs. The knife dropped.

The man sat up, a hand pressed to his side and the Santa Claus face twisted with pain. Lemminkainen looked bewildered. Shea said, 'Walter says this man is not what he seems. Maybe you better make him use his right face.'

Lemminkainen crooned a spell and spat on the man's

head. A sallow young face glowered up sullenly. The hero said, 'So, my cousins of Pohjola send me greeting for my journey! Bow your head, spy of Pohjola.' He drew his broadsword and felt the edge.

'Hey!' said Brodsky, 'you can't just bump the ghee off like that.'

'Wherefore not?' said Lemminkainen.

'He ain't gone up or got his bit or nothing. Where's the law?'

Lemminkainen shook his head in honest puzzlement. 'Piit, you are surely the strangest of men, whose words are without meaning. Spy, will you bow your head, or shall I have the serfs deal with you in their manner?'

Shea said to Pete, 'They don't have judges or trials around here. I told you this guy was the big boss and made his own law.'

Pete shook his head. 'Some connection man,' he said as Lemminkainen's sword whistled through the air. The man's head thumped on the grass in a little fountain of blood.

'Serfs, bury this carrion!' Lemminkainen shouted, then turned towards the visitors from Ohio. Shea noticed that the expression of shrewdness had come back into his eyes.

'You have the gratitude of a hero,' he said to Brodsky. 'Never have I seen a wrestle-hold like that.'

'Jujitsu,' said Pete. 'Any shamus is hep to it.'

'On our trip to far Pohjola you shall go with us and show it.' His eyes swept the group. 'Which of you is so skilled in magic as to have penetrated the false shaping that deceived even me, the master of spells?'

'Why, I guess that was me,' said Bayard. 'Only I'm not skilled in magic at all. Not the way Harold is.'

Shea said, 'Walter, that must be just the reason. That's why Doc Chalmers couldn't get you out of Xanadu, too. And remember how you saw Lemminkainen's mother untying him when none of the rest us of could? You must be too rational or something, so that spells working a change of appearance make no impression on you.' He turned to Lemminkainen. 'This guy would be more help on the trip than all the rest of us put together.'

The hero appeared to be making a convulsive and prodigious effort to think. Finally, he said, 'For your eyes, O Valtarpayart, so be it, since it is not to be concealed that many and strange are the enchantments that beset the road to this land of fog and darkness.'

Six

Under Lemminkainen's direction, the serfs dragged out the largest of four sleds that stood in a shed stacked high with harness and similar gear.

'What do you know!' said Pete Brodsky. 'Is the big shot going to take a sleigh ride?'

'We all are,' said Shea. 'It's the only way they have of travelling here.'

The detective shook his head. 'If I tell them that back at the precinct, they'll think I'm on the snow myself. Why don't they get wised up and use a heap? Say, Shea, maybe we could dope one out for them! It wouldn't have to be no goldplated boiler, just something that would buzz. These jakes always go for the big-sounding show.'

'It wouldn't work here, even if we could build it,' said Shea. 'Any more than your gun. You want to remember that nothing that hasn't been invented yet will.'

He turned to watch the serfs carrying out armfuls of deerskin blankets and vast sacks of food, which they lashed in position with rawhide ropes. Two of them trundled out a keg of beer and added it to the heap. It looked as though the Elk of Hiisi would have his work cut out for him; but, gazing at the gigantic beast, Shea decided that it looked capable of meeting the demand. Lemminkainen bawled orders about the stowing of the gear and warmer clothes for Bayard and Brodsky, whose twentieth-century garments he regarded with unconcealed contempt.

Presently the tasks were done. All the serfs came out of the building and formed in a line, with Lemminkainen's two women in the middle. He kissed them smackingly, shouted the others into the sled, and jumped in himself. It immediately became crowded. As he cracked his whip and the giant reindeer strained forward, the whole line of serfs and women lifted their heads back and burst into a high-pitched doleful chanting. Most of them seemed to have forgotten the words of what they were supposed to be singing, and those who remembered were off key.

'Marry!' said Belphebe. 'Glad am I, Harold, that these farewells do not come often.'

'So am I,' said Shea behind his hand, 'but it gets Lemminkainen. The mug's eyes actually have tears in them!'

'I wish my schnozz was okay again,' said Brodsky. 'I used to could make them fill a bucket with eye-juice when I gave them "Mother Machree".'

'Then I'm rather glad you got the polyp or whatever it is that prevents you doing it now,' said Bayard, and grabbed the side of the sled, as the Elk of Hiisi went into a swinging trot and the sled bounced and skidded along the muddy track northward.

'Now, listen...' began Brodsky, but just at this moment a flying clod of mud from the animal's hooves took him squarely in the face. 'Jesus!' he shouted, then with a glance at Belphebe, 'Write it on the ice, will you, lady? That was such a nut-buster I forgot for a minute that we gotta take what's laid out for us in the Lord's book, even if he throws the whole package at us.'

Lemminkainen turned his head. 'Strange the language of Ouhaio,' he said, 'but if I hit rightly your saying, O Piit, it is that none may escape the course laid down for him.'

'You got it,' said Brodsky.

'Then,' said the hero, 'if one but knew the incantations, one might call forth the spirits of the future to tell what will come of any doing.'

'No, wait . . .' began Brodsky, but Shea said, 'They can in some continua.'

Bayard said, 'It might be worth trying in this one, Harold. If the thought-pattern is right, as you put it, the ability to see consequences might keep us out of a lot of trouble. Don't you think that with your magic . . .'

They hit a stone just then, and Shea collapsed into the

lap of Belphebe, the only member of the party who had been able to find a place to sit in the jouncing sled. It was not that the road was worse than before, but the strain of hanging on and being bumped made it too difficult to talk. The trunks of birch and fir fled past them, close by on both sides, like the palings of a fence, the branches closing off all but fugitive glimpses of the sky overhead. The road zigzagged slightly – not, so far as Shea could determine, for topographic reasons, since the country was flat as an ironing board – because it had never been surveyed. Now and then the forest would clear a little on one side and a farmhouse or a small lake would appear among the trees. Once they met another sled, horse-drawn, and everybody had to dismount and manhandle the vehicles past each other.

At last, as they reached one of the lakes, Lemminkainen reined in his singular draught-animal, said, 'Pause we here a while for eating,' jumped out and began to rummage among the foodbags.

When he had consumed one of the usual Gargantuan snacks, belched and wiped his mouth with the back of his hand, he announced, 'Valtarpayart and Piit, I have allowed you to accompany me on this journey, but learn that for all your arts, you will be worse than useless unless you learn how to fight. I have brought swords for you, and as we take our ease, you shall learn to use them under the greatest master in all Kalevala.'

He dragged a pair of clumsy, two-edged blades out of the baggage and handed one to each, then sat down on a root, evidently prepared to enjoy himself. 'Cut at him, O Valtarpayart!' he said. 'Try to take his head off.'

'Hey!' said Shea, with a glance at the woebegone faces of his companions. 'This won't do. They don't know anything about this business and they're likely to cut each other up. Honest.'

Lemminkainen leaned back. 'Or they learn the swordsman's business, or they go with me no further.'

'But you said they could come. That isn't fair.'

'It is not in our agreement,' said the hero firmly. 'They

came only by my permission, and that has run out. Either they practise with the swords or turn homewards.'

He looked as though he meant it, too, and Shea was forced to admit that legally he was right. But Belphebe said, 'In Faerie, when we would teach young springalds the use of blades without danger to themselves, we use swords of wooden branch.'

After some persuasion, Lemminkainen agreed to accept this as a substitute. The pair were presently whaling away at each other under his scornful correction with single-sticks made from saplings, and lengths of cloth wound round their hands for protection. Bayard was taller and had the better reach; but Brodsky's jujitsu training had made him so quick that several times he rapped his opponent smartly, and at last brought home a backhand blow on the arm that made Bayard drop his stick.

'An arm was lost that time,' said Lemminkainen. 'Ah, well – I suppose not everyone can be such a swordsman and hero as Kaukomieli.'

He turned away to harness up the reindeer again. Belphebe laid a hand on Shea's arm to keep him from reminding the hero of their own little bout.

The afternoon was a repetition of the morning's journey through country that did not change, and whose appearance was becoming as monotonous as the bumping that accompanied their progress. Shea was not surprised when even Lemminkainen wanted to camp early. With Bayard and Brodsky he set about building a triangular lean-to of branches, while Belphebe and the hero wandered off into the woods in search of fresh game for their evening meal.

While they were picking the bones of some birds that resembled a chicken in size and a grouse in flavour, Lemminkainen explained that he had to make this journey to Pohjola because he had learned by magic that they were holding a great wedding feast there and he had not been invited.

'Crashing the party, eh?' said Brodsky. 'I don't get it. Why don't you just give those muzzlers the air?'

'It would decrease my reputation,' said Lemminkainen. 'And besides, there will be a great making of magic. I should undoubtedly lose some of my magical powers if I allowed them to do this unquestioned.'

Belphebe said, 'We have bargained to accompany you, Sir Lemminkainen, and I do not seek to withdraw. But if there are so many present as will be at a great feast, I do not see how even with us four, you are much better than you would be alone.'

Lemminkainen gave a roar of laughter. 'O you maiden, O Pelviipi, you are surely not quickwitted. For all magics there must be a beginning. From you and your bowstring I could raise a hundred archers; from the active Harolainen set in line a thousand swordsmen – but not until you yourselves were present.'

'He's right, kid,' said Shea. 'That's good sympathetic magic. I remember Doc Chalmers giving me a lecture on it once. What have you got there?'

Lemminkainen had picked up several of the long wing and tail feathers from the out-size grouse and was carefully smoothing them out. His face took on the expression of exaggerated foxiness it had worn once or twice before.

'In Pohjola they now surely know that the greatest of heroes and magicians approaches,' he said. 'It is well to be prepared for all encounters with something that can be used.' He tucked the feathers in one of his capacious pockets, glanced at the fire, which was beginning to show brightly in the gathering dusk, and lumbered off to bed.

Bayard said, 'It strikes me, Harold, that the magic in this continuum is quantitatively greater and qualitatively more potent than any you have reported before. And if Lemminkainen can turn you into a thousand swordsmen, can't the other people do something like that? I should say it's rather dangerous.'

'I was just thinking of that,' said Shea, and went to bed himself.

The next day was a repetition of the first, except that

Brodsky and Bayard were so stiff they could barely drag themselves from their deerskin blankets to go through the sword-exercises on which Lemminkainen insisted before breakfast. There was not much conversation in the sled, but when they assembled around the fire in the evening. Lemminkainen entertained them with a narrative of his exploits until Shea and Blephebe wandered off out of earshot.

It was followed by more of the same. On the fifth day, the single-stick practice at noon had progressed so far that Lemminkainen himself took a hand and promptly knocked Brodsky out. It appeared to improve relations all around; the detective took it in good part, and the hero was in the best of humour that evening.

But soon after the start the next morning, he began weaving his head from side to side with a peering expression and sniffing. 'What's the trouble?' asked Shea.

'I smell magic – the strong magic of Pohjola. Look sharp, Valtarpayart.'

They did not have to look very sharp. A glow soon became visible through the trees, which presently opened out to reveal a singular spectacle. Stretching down from the right and losing itself round a turn in the distance, came a depression like a dry river-bed. But instead of water this depression was filled with a fiery red shimmer, and the stones and sand of the bottom were glowing like red-hot metal. On the far side of this phenomenon rose a sharp peak of rock, where sat an eagle as big as a beach-cottage.

As Shea shielded his face against the scorch, the eagle rotated its head and gazed speculatively at the party.

There was no necessity to rein in the Elk of Hiisi. Lemminkainen turned to Bayard. 'What do you see, eyes of Ouhaiola?'

'A red-hot pavement that looks like the floor of Hell, and an eagle several times the size of a natural one. There's a kind of shimmer – no, they're both there, all right.'

The giant bird slowly stretched one wing. 'Oh-oh,' said Shea. 'You were right, Walter. This is . . .'

Belphebe leaped from the sled, tested the wind with an uplifted finger and began to string her bow; Brodsky looked round and round, pugnacious but helpless.

Lemminkainen said, 'Save your arrows, dainty Pelviipi. I myself, the mighty wizard, know a trick worth two of this one.'

The monster eagle leaped into the air. Shea said, 'I hope you know what you're doing, Kauko,' and whipped out his epee, feeling how inadequate it was. It was no longer than one of the bird's talons and nowhere near so thick.

The eagle soared, spiralled upward, and then began to come down on them in a prodigious power dive as Bayard gasped. But Lemminkainen left his own weapon hanging where it was, contenting himself with tossing into the air the feathers of the big grouse, chanting a little staccato ditty whose words Shea could not catch.

The feathers turned themselves into a flock of grouse, which shot off slantwise with a motorcycle whirr. The eagle, almost directly over them – Shea could see the little movements of its wingtips and tail-feathers as it balanced itself on the air – gave a piercing shriek, flapped its wings, and shot off after the grouse. Soon it was out of sight beyond the treetops westward.

'Now it is to be seen that I am not less than the greatest of magicians,' said Lemminkainen, sticking out his chest. 'But this spelling is wearisome work, and there lies before us this river of fire. Harol, you are a wizard. Do you make a spell against it while I restore myself with food.'

Shea stood gazing at the redness and pondered. The glowing flicker had a hypnotic effect, like a dying wood-fire. A good downpour ought to do the trick; he began recalling a rain-spell he and Chalmers had been working up, in the hope of putting down the flaming barrier around Castle Carena during their adventures in the world of the *Orlando Furioso*.

He muttered his spell and made the passes. Nothing happened.

'Well?' said Lemminkainen, with his mouth full of bread and cheese. 'When does the spell begin?'

'I tried,' said Shea, puzzled, 'but . . .'

'Fool of Ouhaiola! Must I teach you your business? How do you expect a spell to work when you do not sing it?'

That's right, thought Shea. He had forgotten that in this Kalevalan magic, song was an indispensible feature. With his own ability at versification, the passes Lemminkainen did not know how to make, and singing, this spell ought to be a humdinger. He lifted his arms for the passes again and sang at the top of his voice.

The spell was a humdinger. As he finished it, something black seemed to loom overhead, and the landscape was instantly blotted out by a shower of soot-lumps as heavy and tenacious as snowflakes. Shea hastily cancelled the spell.

'Truly, a wonderful wizard!' cried Lemminkainen, coughing and trying to slap the clinging stuff from his clothes. 'Now that he has shown us how to make soot of the river of fire, perhaps he will tell us how to bring fog to Pohjola!'

'Nay,' said Belphebe, 'you shall not be so graceless to my lord. I do declare him an approved sorcerer – but not if he must sing, for he cannot carry one note beyond the next.' She reached out one hand comfortingly.

Brodsky said, 'If I could flag down a right croaker to fix my schnozz, maybe we could work something together.'

'I must even do it myself then,' said Lemminkainen. He tossed soot-contaminated beer from his mug, drew a fresh fill from the keg, took a prodigious swig, leaned back, meditated a moment, and sang:

'Ice of Sariola's mountains,
Ice of ten years' snows compacted,
Forged into Turja's glaciers,
Glaciers ever downward flowing,
In the sea with thunder breaking . . .'

For a while it was not clear what he was driving at. Then a shimmering something appeared in the air over the fiery trench, and gradually hardened with a sparkle of colour. A bridge of ice!

But just as Lemminkainen reached the climax of his song which should have materialized the ice and welded it into a solid structure, there was a slip. Down into the trench roared the bridge of ice in fragments, to shatter and hiss and fill the landscape with vapour.

Lemminkainen looked sour and started again. Everyone else held his breath, watching. This time the bridge melted and vanished even before it was completed.

With a yell of rage, Lemminkainen hurled his cap on the ground and danced on it. Bayard laughed.

'You mock me!' screamed the wizard. 'Outland filth!' He snatched up his beer-mug from where he had put it and flung the contents in Bayard's face. There was less than an inch of beer remaining, but even so it was enough to produce a lively display of suds.

'No!' cried Shea, reaching for his epee as Belphebe grabbed her bow.

But instead of leaping up in anger, instead of even wiping the beer from his face, Bayard was staring fixedly at the trench of fire, blinking and knitting his eyebrows. At last he said, 'It's an illusion after all! There isn't anything there but a row of little peat-fires made to look big and only burning in spots. But I don't see how I came to miss it before.'

Shea said, 'Must be the alcohol in the beer. The illusion was so strong that you couldn't see through it until you got the stuff in your eyes. That happened to me once in the continuum of the Norse gods.'

'The spells of Pohjola grow stronger as we approach their stronghold,' said Lemminkainen, his anger forgotten. 'But what counsel shall we take now? For I am too undone with spell-working to undertake the labour of breaking so powerful a magic.'

'We could wait till tomorrow when you'd have your punch back,' suggested Shea.

Lemminkainen shook his head. 'They of Pohjola will surely know what has happened here, and if we are checked by one magic, another and stronger will grow behind, so that at each step the way becomes more impassible. But if now we break through, then their magic becomes weaker.'

'Look here,' said Bayard. 'I think I can resolve this. If you'll give me some beer for eyewash, I can lead the way through. There's plenty of space, even for the sled.'

The Elk of Hiisi snorted and balked, but Lemminkainen was firm with him as Bayard walked ahead, dipping his handkerchief in a mug of beer and applying it to his eyes. Shea found that although he was uncomfortably warm, he was not being cooked as he expected; nor did the sled show any signs of taking fire.

On the far side, they went up a little slope and halted. Bayard started back towards the sled and then halted, pointing at a tall dead pine. 'That's a man!' he cried.

Lemminkainen leaped clumsily from the sled, tugging at his sword, Shea and Brodsky right behind him. As they approached the pine, its branches seemed to collapse with a gentle swoosh; then they were looking at a stocky man of about Lemminkainen's own proportions, his face wearing an expression of sullen bitterness.

'I had thought there must be someone near us for illusion-making,' roared Lemminkainen, happily. 'Bow your head, magician of Pohjola.'

The man looked around quickly and desperately. 'I am Vuohinen the champion, and I challenge,' he said.

'What does he mean?' asked Shea.

'A true champion may always challenge, even in another's house,' said Limmenkainen. 'Whoever wins they take off the head of the other or make him his serf. Which of us do you challenge?'

Vuohinen the champion looked from one to the other and pointed to Bayard. 'This one. What is his art?'

'No,' said Lemminkainen, 'for his art is the seeing eye that penetrates all magics, and if you challenge him, you have already lost, since he penetrated your disguise. You may have Harol here, with the point-sword – or the shield-maiden Pelviipi with the bow, or Piit in wrestle, or myself with the broadsword.' He grinned.

Vuohinen looked from one to the other. 'Of the point-sword I know nothing,' he said, 'and while there is doubtless no bowman in the world half as good as myself, I have other uses for women than slaying them. I choose Piit in open wrestle.'

'And not the lively Kaukomieli!' said Lemminkainen with a laugh. 'You think you have chosen safely. But you shall see what unusual arts lie among the outland friends of Kalevala. Will you wrestle with him, Piit?'

'Okay,' said Brodsky, and began shucking his shirt. Vuohinen already had his off.

They circled, swinging their arms like a pair of indifferently educated apes. Shea noticed that Vuohinen's arms reminded him of the tyres of a semi-trailer truck, and the detective looked puny beside him. Then Vuohinen jumped and grabbed. Brodsky caught him by the shoulders and threw himself backwards, placing the sole of his foot against Vuohinen's midriff and shoving upwards as he fell, so that his antagonist flew over him and landed heavily on his back.

Lemminkainen gave a bellow of laughter. 'I will make a song about this!' he shouted.

Vuohinen got up somewhat slowly and scowling. This time he came in more cautiously, then when at arm's length from Brodsky, suddenly threw himself at the detective, the fingers of his left hand spread straight for the other's eyes. Shea heard Belphebe gasp, but even as she gasped, Brodsky jerked his head back, and with a quickness wonderful to behold, seized the thumb of the clawing hand in one of his, the little finger in the other and, bracing himself, twisted powerfully.

There was a crack; Vouhinen pinwheeled through the air and came down on his side, then sat up, his face contorted with pain, feeling with the other hand of a wrist and fingers that hung limp.

'There was a creep in Chi tried to pull that rat caper on

me once,' said Brodsky pleasantly. 'Want any more, or have you got the chill?'

'It was a trick,' Vuohinen bleated. 'With a sword . . .'

Lemminkainen stepped forward cheerfully. 'Do you wish his head as trophy or himself to serve you daily?'

'Aw,' said Brodsky, 'I suppose he ain't much use as a patsy with that busted duke, but let's let him score for the break. The pastor would put the run on me if I hit him with the lily.' He walked over to Vuohinen and kicked him deliberately. 'That's for the rat caper. Get up!'

Vouhinen made the sled more crowded than ever and, as Brodsky had said, was of no great value as a servant, but he did make lighter the job of collecting firewood in the evening. Moreover, Brodsky's victory had improved relations with Lemminkainen. He still insisted that Bayard practise daily with the detective – they were at the point where they used real swords now – but now the hero himself practised jujitsu falls and holds and tumbles almost daily. He was an apt pupil, too.

Around the travellers the air was colder; plumes of vapour appeared at their nostrils and those of the reindeer. The sun never seemed to break through the overcast any more. The trees became sparser and stunted, growing scattered among little grassy hillocks. Sometimes Belphebe brought home no game at all in the evening. More often than not, it would be two or three rabbits, which sent Lemminkainen back to the stored provisions after he had eaten his share.

Still the sled bumped and slid along the muddy track northward, until one afternoon, as they came over a little hill from behind a group of trees, Lemminkainen cried, 'Great Jumala! Look at that!'

Before them, stretching out of sight in both directions a prodigious fence ran across the valley. A row of palings, less than a foot apart and reaching almost to the low cloud canopy; but it was the sight of the horizontal members that really made Shea's scalp prickle. For the palings were bound together by an immense mass of snakes, wound together in and out, though whether they got that way because they wanted to or because someone had tied them in that grotesque fashion, it was impossible to tell.

As the sled slid up, the reindeer shying and trembling, the snakes turned their heads towards the party and began hissing like a thousand tea-kettles.

'It must be an illusion,' said Bayard, 'though at present I can't see anything but that mass of serpents. Give me some beer.'

Lemminkainen drew some of the fluid from the cask. Vuohinen's face held a sneer of triumph. The reason was apparent as soon as Bayard dabbed the liquid in his eyes, stared at the remarkable fence again, and shook his head.

'They still look like serpents to me,' he said. 'I know it can't be true, but there they are.'

Shea said, 'Couldn't we just assume they're fakes and cut our way through?'

Lemminkainen shook his head. 'Learn, O Harol of Ouhaio, that within this field of magic everything has all the powers of its seeming unless its true name be known.'

'I see. And we're now right into Pohjola, where their magic is really strong. You couldn't try a spell yourself to take this one off, whatever it is?'

'Not unless I know the real name beneath this false seeming,' said the hero.

'Maybe we can play it straight,' said Shea, and turning to Belphebe, 'How about trying a shot with your bow at one of those beasties? The way I understand it, if you killed one, it would have to return to its proper form.'

'Not so, O Harolainen,' said Lemminkainen. 'It would be a dead serpent merely until we learned its true form. And there are thousands.'

They gazed at the spectacle for a moment or two. It was fairly revolting, but the snakes made no movement to leave their position.

Suddenly Pete Brodsky said, 'Hey! I got a idea.'

'What is it?' asked Shea.

Brodsky jerked a thumb towards Vuohinen. 'This

gummy belongs to me, don't he?'

'Under the laws of this country, I believe that's right,' said Shea, and 'He is your serf,' said Lemminkainen.

'And he's on this magic lay in this joint?'

Shea said, 'Why, so he is, now that you mention it. He must have been the one who worked the river of fire and the eagle.'

Brodsky reached a hand out and grabbed Vuohinen by the collar. 'All right, punk! What's the right name for them potato-water dreams out there?'

'Awk!' said Vuohinen. 'Never will I be a traitor . . .'

'Bag your head on that stuff. Come across with the right dope, or I'll have shorty here let you have it.' He pointed significantly to the sword that hung at Lemminkainen's side.

'Awk!' said Vuohinen again, as the hand twisted in his collar. 'They are – made from lingonberries.'

Walter Bayard said, 'Why, so they are!' He walked across to the hissing, snarling barrier, reached out his hand, twisted the head off one of the serpents, and ate it.

Lemminkainen laughed. 'Now there will be a removing of spells, and then we shall have lingonberry dessert to our meal. I thank you, friend Piit.'

Seven

The lingonberry wall came down to a tangled mat of vegetation under Lemminkainen's ministrations and they camped just beyond. The hero was in hilarious humour, making a series of jokes which nobody but Brodsky found diverting and shouting with laughter over his own sallies, until Shea said, 'For the love of Mike, Kauko, what's got into you tonight? You sound as though you had just won the first prize.'

'And have I not, Harol? For I know well that we are through the last barrier that Louhi can throw against us, and tommorow we shall arrive at Pohjola's hall – perhaps to fight.'

Shea said, 'I can see that would be just about the best thing that ever happened.'

He himself didn't feel the same way, not even in the morning when they began to sight tilled fields with a few domestic animals. Presently there was a stead of considerable size visible among the tops of the low trees. Lemminkainen clucked at the Elk of Hiisi, and the giant reindeer pulled up beside a slow stream that wound across the featureless landscape.

The hero dug into the duffel at the rear of the sled for his shirt of scale-mail and put it on. 'For you, my friends,' he said, 'I have brought armour second in quality only to my own.'

He dragged out four sleeveless hip-length jackets of a double thickness of leather, tanned so stiff that Shea found it was all he could do to get into the thing. It was just as heavy as a well-made steel cuirass would have been, far more clumsy and less effective, but he supposed the metallurgy of Kalevala would not be up to such an article. Belphebe wriggled out of hers almost as soon as she was in it. 'Marry,' she said, 'you may keep your beetle's bodice, Sir Lemminkainen. I shall need free arms if I'm to go to war.'

Lemminkainen produced for each of them a skull-cap of the same thick leather, with a strip of iron around the rim and a pair of semi-circular strips that sprang from it to meet at the top of the wearer's head. These fitted better, though Brodsky's gave him the odd effect of wearing a rimless derby hat.

They climbed back into the sled. The Elk of Hiisi splashed across the little stream towards a group of buildings. Brodsky pointed, 'These Hoosiers sure play it for the works. Look at them sconces!'

Shea saw that a nearby hillock was decorated with a row of stakes – about fifty, he judged – each stake surmounted by a severed human head. The heads were in various stages of decrepitude; only one stake, at the end of the line, lacked its gruesome ornament. A score of ravens flew croaking up from the heads as they approached and Bayard remarked, 'I'm glad there's only one vacancy.'

Vuohinen said sourly, 'You will soon learn how little the stakes of Pohjola are exhausted.'

Lemminkainen pivoted round, hit him a solid back-hand blow on the ear, and said, 'Now my friends, you shall see that the handsome Kaukomieli is not less skilful with magic than he is with the sword.'

He brought the reindeer to a halt, leaped to the ground and, pulling a number of twigs from the stunted trees, began arranging them in rows, crooning to himself. Presently there were enough twigs to satisfy him; he stepped back, and his voice rose higher as he made a series of passes with his hands. Shea could see that they were sound magic, of a type he had seen in other space-time continua, but the hero moved too rapidly for him to follow the precise pattern. Then there was a little rush of air and, where the first twig had been, Shea was looking at a replica of himself, complete with epee, leather jacket, and ironbound cap.

Another, and another, and another Shea flashed into being, a whole row of Harold Sheas, who at once began to crowd round the sled.

Belphebe gave a little squeal. 'Am I wed to all of these?' she cried. But, as she did so, the quota of Sheas was apparently filled up, and Belphebes began to leap from the ground where Lemminkainen had arranged his twigs. They mingled with the simulacra of Shea as the magician's voice went up one more tone, and copies of Brodsky joined the growing crowd, shaking hands and clapping one another on the back.

Lemminkainen's song came to an end; the sled was surrounded by at least a hundred replicas of the three. In it remained one Lemminkainen, one sour-looking Vuohinen, and a single Bayard. Bayard said, 'A brilliant piece of work, Lemminkainen, but could these reproductions actually cut somebody up, or are they phantoms? They look all right to me, but I haven't tried it with beer in my eye.'

'Seek to wrestle with one of these Piits, and you shall see,' said Lemminkainen. 'They will have all the strength of life unless someone finds which is the real one and which the shadow and make a counter-spell, using the true name of the one.'

'Wait a minute,' said Bayard. 'Haven't we got someone here who can identify all these people for the Pohjolans?' He pointed at Vuohinen.

'By the mill!' said Lemminkainen. 'It is clear that I am wise as well as brave, for no one else would have thought to bring on this journey a person so capable of seeing through millstones as yourself. Piit, Harol, Pelviipi, you must mingle with your other selves and let some of those other selves come upon the sled, lest these people of Turja find the true ones.'

Shea stared a second, then said to Belphebe: 'He's right, kid. See you later.' He squeezed her hand and jumped over the side into the mob. Walter came with him. 'I don't want to lose sight of the real one myself,' he said.

Behind them, three or four Brodskys tried to climb into

the sled at once. The one who made it first promptly kicked Vuohinen. 'Get wise, punk,' he said. 'Pull any fast ones on me, and I'll let you have it.'

Shea observed that, while the various Brodskys had formed a compact group to march behind the sled, chattering with each other, most of the reproductions of himself and Belphebe had paired off. One of the unengaged ones sidled up to him and pressed his hand. It couldn't be the real one, and yet her touch was as cool and her step as light as though it were. It occurred to him that unless someone pronounced the counter-spell fairly soon, some neat marital problems would arise in a continuum that contained about thirty-five Sheas and as many Belphebes, all presumably supplied with the due quota of emotions.

Bayard said, 'There's one point, Harold. It seems to me that it should be possible to tell within easily determinable limits how our presence here will affect the outcome of the epic. We have all the elements. We know what happened in the original story, and we have fairly accurate information about ourselves. It seems to me that an equation could be set up . . .'

'Yeah, for one of those electronic thinking machines,' said Shea. 'Only we don't happen to have one, and if we did, it wouldn't work.'

'There was a witch once in Faerie,' said the Belphebe by his side, 'that warned people from danger after she had looked in a pool by magic and seen to where a course would lead.'

'That's what I mean,' said Bayard. 'Apparently you can do things by magic in this continuum that a calculating machine couldn't think of equalling. Now if before we start something – say going into that hall there – we found out it was going to turn out badly, then we could change it to the right kind of future by taking another action.'

'That's a bum steer,' said one of the Brodskys, who had fallen into step with them. 'Get smart, will you? Everything that's gonna happen has been put on the line by God ever since the clock began to tick. It says so in the Bible.'

'Listen, my predestinarian friend,' said Bayard, 'I shall be glad to prove the contrary . . .'

'Not with magic,' said Shea. 'You're the only one it doesn't affect now, and if you got to working spells, you might lose your immunity. Hey, they've spotted us.'

A man was running, shouting, towards one of the buildings from which came sounds of revelry. The door of this building opened as the sled came to a stop, and several broad, black-bearded faces appeared in the opening. Shea saw one of the other Sheas put an arm around a Belphebe and felt a quite illogical pang of jealousy over the thought that this might be the real one.

Lemminkainen jumped out of the sled, followed by a Shea, a Belphebe and a Brodsky, who clamped a wrist-lock on Vuohinen. Men began to file out of the hall and stand opposite the company of visitors, who drew up in a rough line. They looked much like other Kalevalans, though perhaps even shorter and with more Mongoloid faces. They were armed and looked thoroughly unpleasant. Shea felt a prickling at the back of his neck and loosened his epee in its scabbard.

But Lemminkainen looked unimpressed. 'Hail, my cousins of Pohjola!' he said. 'Do you wish to keep me standing here outside the hall of feasting?'

Nobody answered him; instead, more of them came frowning out. Lemminkainen turned.

'Fair Pelviipi,' he said, 'show them your art, that they may learn how silly it is to oppose the friends of the heroic Kaukomieli.'

As though actuated by a single brain, thirty-five Belphebes, placed one foot each against the ends of their bows and snapped the strings into place. Like so many Rockettes, they each placed an arrow on the string, took one pace back, and looked around for a target. One of the ravens from the palisade of heads chose that moment to come flapping over, with a loud 'Kraw-k.'

Thirty-five bowstrings twanged; the raven came tumbling downward, looking like a pincushion, transfixed by all the arrows that could find room in its carcass. 'Nice work, kid,' said Shea, before he realized he was talking to a simulacrum.

It impressed the Pohjolans, too. There was a quick, low-toned gabbling among them, and a couple disappeared inside. In a moment they were back and the company began to disappear through the door. Lemminkainen said, 'Follow me!' and stamped up behind them. Shea hurried, not wishing to be left outside, and reached the door simultaneously with the Shea who had been in the sled.

'Sorry,' said the other Shea, 'but I came here to go to this party with my wife.'

'She's my wife, too,' said Shea, grabbing a Belphebe at random and leading her through the door behind the other couple. Thank Heaven, there were enough of them to go round.

Inside, several rushlights flickered. A fire blazed on the central hearth, to some extent counteracting the inadequate illumination characteristic of Kalevalan houses. The whole long hall was crowded with benches and tables, at which sat scores of men and quite a few women. All heads were turned towards the newcomers.

Shea's eyes followed Lemminkainen's towards the centre of the hall, where a table with some space about it was apparently the place of honour. At it sat the tallest Kalevalan Shea had ever seen; this was undoubtedly the bridegroom. There was a sharp-featured, snag-toothed, muscular-looking woman – Louhi, the Mistress of Pohjola, no doubt. The stout man with his eyes drooping sleepily and a mug of drink before him must be the Master of Pohjola. The girl with the fancy beaded headdress was probably the bride. Louhi's daughter.

The duplicate Shea touched him on the arm. 'Even nicer dish than Kylliki, isn't she?' he whispered. It was odd to have one's own thoughts come back at one out of one's own mouth.

Lemminkainen strode to the nearest bench, reached out and pitched the last man on it to the floor. Then he slammed his muddy boot down on the bench and shouted:

'Greetings to you on my coming.
Greetings also to the greeter!
Hearken, Pohjola's great Master,
Have ye here within this dwelling.
Beer to offer to the hero?'

Louhi dug her elbow into her husband's ribs. He forced his eyes open, gave a grunt and replied, 'If you care to stand quietly over there in the corner, between the kettles, where the hoes are hanging, we will not prevent you.'

Lemminkainen laughted, but it was an angry laugh. 'Seems to me that I'm unwelcome,' he chanted:

'As no ale is offered to me,
To the guest who has just entered.'

'No guest you,' cried Louhi, 'but a trouble-making boy, not fit to sit among your elders. Well, if you seek trouble, by Ukko, you shall find it!'

'Yes?' said Lemminkainen, sitting down heavily on the bench.

'Pohjola's illustrious Mistress,
Long-toothed Mistress of Pimentola,
Thou hast held the wedding badly,
And in doggish fashion held it . . .'

He chanted on, comparing Louhi to various species of unpleasant fauna and extending the compliments to most of her guests. There seemed to be a routine about this sort of thing, Shea decided; the others merely sat, waiting till Lemminkainen had finished.

Behind him he heard the duplicate Shea say to Bayard,

'All right, I admit it might work, and it's within the laws of magic. But if anybody's going to try it, you better let me. You just haven't had enough experience with it, Walter.'

He whirled. 'What might work?'

His twin said, 'Walter's been watching Lemminkainen, and thinks he's worked out a magical method for determining the future results of a given series of events.'

'I just want to show up this predestination business for . . .' began Bayard.

'Sssh,' said the duplicate Shea. 'They've finished saying hello. Here comes the floor show.'

The Master of Pohjola had at last opened his eyes fully and was chanting a spell. In the space between the table of honour and the hearth, there appeared a pool of water. The Master cried:

'Here's a river thou mayst drink of,
Here's a pool that thou mayst splash in!'

'Ha, ha!' bellowed Lemminkainen.
'I'm no calf by women driven,
Nor a bull with tail behind me,
That I drink of river water,
Or of filthy ponds the water.'

His tone went lower, and without apparent effort he sang up an enormous ox, under whose hooves the floor creaked alarmingly. The ox, after a vague look around the company, began schlooping up the water by the bucketful.

Shea said to his Belphebe, 'Probably brought up in somebody's parlour, so he doesn't think a thing about it.'

The Master of Pohjola was already at work on a new spell. Its result was a great grey wolf, which took one look at the ox and bounded towards it. The ox gave a bawl of terror, whirled, and thundered towards the door, while the Pohjolans fell over one another to get out of the way. It plunged through, taking part of the doorframe with it, and vanished, with the wolf right behind.

Louhi sneered. 'You are vanquished in the contest of magic, O Kaukomieli! Now begone, or ever worse come upon you.'

'No man who deserves the name would let himself be driven from any place where he chose to stay,' said Lemminkainen, 'least of all a hero like myself. I challenge.'

The Master stood up. He moved lightly for so beefy an individual. 'Let us then measure our swords together to see which is the better.'

Lemminkainen grinned and drew his broadsword. 'Little of my sword is left me, for on bones it has been shattered. But come, let us measure them.'

The Master crossed over to the wall and took his sword from a peg. The Belphebe next to Shea said, 'Shall I notch a shaft?'

'I don't think so,' he replied. 'It's not likely to turn into a general riot unless somebody breaks the rules. They're too nervous about those bows.'

The contenders were measuring their swords in the cleared space. From where he stood, it seemed to Shea that the Master's was a trifle longer. The guests crowded forward to watch, while those behind yelled to them to sit down. At last the Master ordered them back to their seats.

'And you newcomers, too!' he shouted. 'Back against the wall!'

That seemed to remind Lemminkainen of something. He said, 'Before that we work out our challenge, I will challenge any present – to the point-sword against my companion Harol, or to the wrestle with my companion Piit. It will be rare sport to watch, after I have disposed of you.'

The duplicate Shea said, 'Isn't he generous?' But one of the Belphebes put her hand on his arm and he felt better.

'You will be watching no more sports,' said the Master. 'Are you ready?'

'I am ready,' said Lemminkainen.

The Master leaped forward, swinging his sword up for a tremendous overhand cut, as if he were serving a tennis ball. The blow was never completed, however, for the swordblade struck a rafter overhead with a loud chunk. Lemminkainen made a pass at his opponent, who leaped backward with wonderful agility.

Lemminkainen roared with laughter, saying, 'What has the rafter done to you, that you should punish it? But that is always the way with little men when confronted by a true hero. Come, there's too little room in here. And do you not think that your blood would look prettier on the grass outside?'

He turned and shouldered his way towards the door. As Shea followed him, Leminkainen leaned close and, with his foxy expression, whispered, 'I think that some of them are false seemings. Let your friend Payart watch sharply.'

Before Shea could reply, the others were coming. Outside, the phantom company sat or stood on the grass, talking. Shea wondered whether, when the spell came off, he would find himself remembering what the others had said. He wished he had Doc Chalmers around; there were times when this magic business got pretty complicated for an incomplete enchanter.

The Master and Lemminkainen halted in the yard, between the main house and the hillock with its head-decorated row of stakes. A couple of serfs brought a big cowhide, which they laid on the grass to provide securer footing. Lemminkainen took his stance at one edge of it, stamping his feet to test the give of the hide. He jerked his thumb towards the heads, saying, 'When we finish, that last stake will no longer feel ashamed of its nakedness. Are you ready?'

'I am ready,' said the Master of Pohjola.

Shea glanced at his companions. The version of Belphebe nearest him was watching with an intent, studious expression that showed duels were nothing particularly new to her. One of the Brodskys said, 'Shea, this may be for the monkeys, but these birds are no flukers. If we could make TV with this show, there'd be enough scratch in it to . . .'

'Sh!' said Bayard. 'I'm concentrating.'

Clang! went the blades, the Master of Pohjola forcing the attack. His longer blade flashed overhand, forehand, backhand. 'Wonderful wrists,' said one of the phantom Sheas. Lemminkainen, not giving an inch, was parrying every swing. There was little footwork in this style of sword-play. They faced each other squarely, hewing as if trying to fell trees, pausing occasionally for a rest, then slashing away again.

Once the Master's blade came down on Lemminkainen's shoulder, but at a slight angle, so that the scale-mail slipped the blow aside. Then Lemminkainen got in a cut at the Master's neck that the latter did not quite parry in time. Blood trickled from a small cut.

'Ho, ho!' cried Lemminkainen. 'Hearken, Master of Pohjola, true it is, your neck so wretched is as red as dawn of morning!'

The Master, stepping back half a pace, rolled his eyes downward for a fraction of a second as though to assess the damage. Instantly Lemminkainen, advancing so fast that Shea could not quite see how he did it, struck again. The blade went right through the Master's neck. The head, turning over in the air, fell in a graceful parabola, and the body, half-twisting as the legs buckled under it, fell spouting upon the cowhide. There was a gasping groan from the crowd. Louhi shrieked.

Lemminkainen, grinning until it seemed as though his mouth must meet behind, like Humpty-Dumpty's, cried: 'So much for the heroes of Pohjola!'

He stepped forward, wiped his blade with care on the trousers of the corpse, and sheathed it. Then he picked up the head and strutted to the empty stake.

'Now, wicked wretches, fetch me beer!' he bellowed.

Shea turned to say something to the nearest Belphebe. It was not until that moment that he remembered Bayard had said, '*I'm concentrating*.' He turned around and looked. Sure enough, there was Bayard, his back to the arresting spectacle of Lemminkainen's victory march, crouched on the ground over a little pile of grasses. He seemed to be muttering to himself; a tiny curl of smoke came from the pile.

'Walter, no!' shouted Shea, and dived for him.

Too late.

There was a little flash of fire, a sound of displaced air, and in an instant all the duplicate Sheas, Belphebes and Brodskys had vanished. As Shea and Bayard rolled over together, they heard Lemminkainen's shout, 'Fool! Bungler! Traitor! Your spell has cancelled mine. The agreement is ended!'

Shea pulled himself to his knees in time to see the hero walking, not running, towards the sled with his sword out. Nobody seemed anxious to be the first to stop him.

Down towards the edge of what had been the Pohjolan cheering section around the combatants, there was a half-muffled cry, and out of a struggling group projected a leg, dainty even in the shapeless garment.

'Belphebe!' shouted Shea, getting to his feet and tugging at his sword with the same motion. Before he could get the epee out of its scabbard, he too went down under a swarm of bodies. He had just time to notice that they didn't bath often enough and that Brodsky had laid out one of the assailants with a neat crack of his black-jack, and then he was hopelessly pinioned, being marched along beside Bayard.

'Put them in the strong-house!' said the Mistress of Pohjola. Her face did not look as though she intended it to be a place of entertainment.

As the captives were frog-marched along, Shea saw the Elk of Hiisi retreating into the distance, with the sled bouncing along behind him.

Eight

The four were tumbled unceremoniously over each other on to a stone floor. Shea heard a massive door slam, and the clash as several large bolts were driven home behind them. He got up and pulled Belphebe to her feet.

'Are you hurt, kid?' he asked.

'Nay, not I.' She rubbed one wrist where someone's grip had come down hard. 'But there are places I would rather be.'

'It's a real jook-joint, all right,' said Brodsky. 'You got me on how we're going to push a can from this one.'

He was looking around the place in the dim illumination furnished by the single, eight-inch window, which was heavily barred. The stronghouse itself was composed of massive tree-trunks, and its roof seemed abnormally thick.

'Alackaday,' said Belphebe. 'What happened to those shapings of ourselves that so confounded these gentry but lately?'

'Walter took care of that,' said Shea. 'I admit I'm just as glad to have only one wife, but he was a little precipitate. What in hell were you up to, Walter?'

Bayard said, 'I was merely trying in a small way to carry out the plan I mentioned of divining the future. It worked, too.'

'What do you mean, it worked?' said Shea.

'I was trying to find out who would win the duel. There were little fiery letters on the ground that said "Lem" as clearly as could be.'

'A big help,' said Shea, 'especially as he took off the other guy's head about that time, anyway.'

Bayard said, 'The principle is established. And how was I to know it would counteract Lemminkainen's spell? Nobody warned me of any such outcome. What is the logical nexus between the two, by the way?'

Shea shrugged. 'I haven't the least idea. Maybe we can work it out sometime when we have the leisure. But in the meanwhile, we need to figure out some plan for getting out of here. These people don't fool around at any time, and that old witch has just lost her husband.'

He went to the little window and looked out. Or tried to, for he found his vision blocked by a familiar-looking bewhiskered countenance: Vuohinen, who spat through the bars at him.

Shea dodged, wiped his shoulder with the cuff of the other hand, and turned to Brodsky. 'Pete, he's your serf. Maybe you can order him . . .'

'Ha!' roared Vuohinen. 'This one to order me? I am free of all serfdom now, and have been charged to see that you outlandish tricksters do not escape before the Mistress of Pohjola undertakes your punishment.'

'What do you mean?'

'All details I do not know, but be assured it will be a memorable occasion. She is like to have you flayed and rolled in salt, to be followed by slow burning.'

Shea fell back and looked around. Whoever had planned this box had built for keeps. The massive simplicity of the structure would defy any amount of tinkering. For instance, there was no opening whatever on the inside of the door through which one could get at the outside.

'I know your names!' shouted Vuohinen from the window. 'Your wizardries will have no power on me.'

He was probably right, at that. But an idea occurred to Shea. He returned to the window. 'Look here,' he said. 'I'm a champion and I challenge you.'

Vuohinen shook his head. 'I am no longer a champion myself since losing the wrestle to this Piit, and cannot take your challenge until he has been beheaded.'

'Wait a minute,' said Bayard, 'if . . .'

'Ya!' said Vuohinen. 'I see your plot. Be known that I shall take care that your head comes off first, and his the last of all.' He turned his back and walked away from the window.

Shea turned to Brodsky. 'Pete, you should know a lot about busting out of places like this. What do the chances look like to you?'

Brodsky, who had been moving slowly around the cell, poking and testing, shook his head. 'This is a real tough can. It would be a soup job, and even then there'd be the strong-arm squad out there to play.'

Bayard said: 'Couldn't we lure Vuohinen up to the bars and then grab him and choke him?'

'No good,' said Brodsky. 'What do you get except a good feeling in your biscuit? He ain't got no keys.'

Belphebe said, 'Yet while you are an approved sorcerer, Harold, it seems to me that we are not utterly without resource.' She took her turn at stepping to the window. 'Ohe, Vuohinen,' she called.

'What now, female toad?'

'I understand how you are angry with us. We were lacking in sympathy, in not thinking of the damage to your hand. But we will make amends. If you will tell us somewhat of yourself, my lord, who knows no little magic, will make it good for you.'

Shea squeezed her hand. 'Nice try, kid,' he said under his breath. But Vouhinen saw the point, too.

'And put myself in his power? Ya, the hand will heal itself quickly enough when I see your heads on stakes.'

Shea took over with, 'You're a pretty tough guy, aren't you?'

'That I am.'

'Yes, sir,' said Shea. 'Some of them are good where I come from, but for plain toughness, I'm afraid we're not in your class. Must be the diet or something. How did you get that way, anyway?'

'Ya,' said Vuohinen, 'you seek by flattery to disarm me, so that you may persuade me to let you go. I am not so simple.'

Bayard said, 'He seems to be up on psychology, too, doesn't he?'

Shea sighed. 'Psychology worked in the world of Norse myth when I got thrown in the jug.'

'The trouble seems to be,' said Bayard, 'that this animal is a Finn. In our own world the Finns are about the stubbornest race on earth, like the Dutch and maybe the Basques. There's something in the culture-pattern. I don't think you're going to get anywhere with him . . . I wonder how much time we have left?'

Belphebe said, 'Harold, my love, I think the answer stares us in the face, but we have so looked at small details as to miss the great. Why cannot we leave this whole world of Kalevala by the same door we entered in: item, your symbolic magic?'

Shea slapped his thigh. 'Just the thing! Wait a minute, though . . . Any kind of magic in this continuum takes a lot of music, and I guess my voice just isn't equal to it. That's why I've had trouble so far.'

'Alas, I fear I can do but little more for you,' said Belphebe. 'Not that I croak like you, my love, but my voice is so slender. I could attune a harp if we had such a thing. Timias, my fiancé in Faerie, taught me the art.'

Bayard shook his head. Brodsky said, 'Not that I want to noise off, but if my schnozz was on the up-and-up . . .'

Shea said, 'Wait a minute here. I think I see a way. Have you ever had that polyp taken out, Pete?'

'Naw.'

'Why not?'

'I been busy . . . And besides, I don't want no croaker putting me through the mill.' His voice was defensive, but Shea rushed on. 'Well, why don't we begin by curing your polyp by magic? That ought not to take much of a spell, and if your voice were working right, we could tackle something harder.'

'Say, maybe you got a right steer there. But how are you going to wrap it up without music?'

'I think that Belphebe's voice with the help of a harp ought to be enough for the smaller spell. Then she could accompany you, and I'll work out the big one. Wait, I'll try.'

He stepped to the window again. 'Oh, Vuohinen!'

'Well, what now?'

'Do you know what a kantele is?'

'What child does not?'

'Good. Could you get us one to lighten our last hours?'

'Why should I lighten your last hours, filth?' He turned away again.

Shea sighed again. 'No co-operation – that's the trouble with this damned continuum,' he said.

Bayard asked, 'What's a kantele?'

'The primitive harp. Vainamoinen invented it at some point in the runes, by making it out of a fish's jawbone, but I wasn't sure he'd done it yet, so I asked this guy if he knew what it was.'

'If we had a fish's jawbone . . .'

'We could make one ourselves. Yes, I know. But our chances of getting a fish's jawbone out of that big lump of insensitivity are about as good as those of biting our way through those logs.'

'I can fix that,' said Brodsky, suddenly.

'Oh, yeah?' said Shea, and 'Can you, indeed?' said Bayard, both together.

'Oh, yeah,' said Brodsky firmly, and strode to the window again. 'Hey, lug!' he called. 'So you're going to clip our pumpkins tomorrow. Okay. But where's the kiss-off banquet?'

'What use is food to you, who will so soon be beyond the need of it?'

'That's right, play it dumb, lug. Listen we're from Ohio, see? In our country, when a ghee doesn't get what he wants for his last meal, his ghost comes back on the roach that turned him down, and pretty soon the muzzler is playing with the squirrels.'

'It is a lie,' said Vuohinen, but he turned his head from side to side to look at the others, and Shea felt his heart leap. He nodded solemnly in support of the detective. 'That's right,' said Bayard.

'Boy!' said Brodsky gleefully. 'Am I going to get a bang

out of watching you cut off your own toes?'

'Maybe we could make him take off his nose and ears, too, while we're about it,' said Shea.

'That's the dope,' Brodsky continued. 'None of them fried pigs' ears, either. It's gotta be fish, or else.'

The head disappeared. Shea turned to Brodsky. 'You're a better psychologist than I am. How did you know that would fetch him?'

'Ah, I never saw the gorilla yet that didn't fall for the yudd racket,' said Brodsky, modestly. 'They're so afraid of going wack, they'd rather turn themselves in.'

He seemed to have struck oil. Outside there was the sound of feet and a murmur of voices. Then there was a wait, the bolts were drawn back, and the door opened to show Vuohinen, surrounded by a phalanx of the black-bearded Pohjolan warriors. He bore a big wooden platter.

'I told the Mistress of your outlandish custom,' he said, 'and though she says her magic is strong enough for any protection, she will grant you so much.'

He slammed down the platter and stamped out. Shea bent to examine the platter. There was no doubt that it was fish, and more than a little on the high side, some large member of the salmon tribe. He said, 'Well, here's our harp. Walter, help me get the jawbones out of this critter's head.'

'What with? They took all our knives and things.'

'With your fingernails. We can't be squeamish. Ssh, let me think. I'll have to work out the verse for Belphebe.'

'Now,' said Shea, 'can you break off a few hairs, sweetheart?'

Belphebe complied. Shea undertook to tie the strands of hair, one at a time, to the jawbone, so that they spanned its gap like the strings of a harp. In the dim light, it took some doing.

She touched the strings and bent her head close. 'It's awfully small and weak,' she said. 'I don't know.'

'I thought of that,' said Shea. 'Listen carefully, kid, and memorise after me, because you'll have to do it all yourself. Keep your voice way down, as though you were crooning, to match the harp. I'll make the passes, just to be on the safe side, though they may not be necessary.'

Belphebe seated herself on the floor, with the harp on her uplifted knees, cocked her ear down towards it, and began:

'Oh, you harp of fish's jawbone,
Hail, you kantele of magic . . .'

while Shea ran rapidly through some of the passes he had used in Faerie. She was from there, and it would probably help. Belphebe ended:

'. . . be you forthwith ten times greater.'

And fell over on her back as a five-foot harp of fish's jawbone pushed her off balance. Shea helped her up, and she began testing the strings. 'It needs tuning.'

'All right, you tune it, while I work out a verse for that polyp. Pete, what's the name of your wife, and what church do you go to?'

In a few moments they were ready. Pete placed himself before the couple, Belphebe twanged the strings of her harp, and in her light, clear soprano sang the spell for the removal of the polyp.

Brodsky cried, 'Ouch! Damn near took my sconce off.' He felt his nose and a smile spread across his face in the semi-darkness. (Outside the summer day was just ending.) 'Say, Shea . . .'

Whatever he was going to say was never said. The window turned dark, and all four looked up to see Vuohinen's face peering in, bearded and furious.

'Where did you get that?' he shouted. 'Magic! Magic! I know your names! I will . . .' The face abruptly disappeared.

'Sing!' cried Shea to Brodsky. 'Sing anything you can think of! Quick! I'll take care of the sorites. Belphebe, you accompany him, and Walter hold one of his hands.

Now if the class A . . .'

Pete Brodsky tilted his head back, and in a tenor that would have done credit to John McCormack, burst into:

'My wi-ild I-rish rose,
The swe-etest flower that grows . . .'

Outside, beneath the piercing tenor and the twanging of the harp, there was a sound of distant shouting and running feet.

'You may look everywhere . . .'

The walls of the cabin seemed to turn round and round as though they were on a pivot and only the four in the centre fixed in position. And as Pete's voice rose higher and higher, the solid walls turned grey and dissolved, and with them the whole world of the Kalevala.

THE GREEN MAGICIAN

Nine

In that suspended moment when the grey mists began to whirl around them, Harold Shea realised that, although the pattern was perfectly clear, the details often didn't work out right.

It was all very well to realise that, as Doc Chalmers once said, 'The world we live in is composed of impressions received through the senses, and if the senses can be attuned to receive a different series of impressions, we should infallibly find ourselves living in another of the infinite number of possible worlds.' It was a scientific and personal triumph to have proved that, by the use of the sorites of symbolic logic, the gap to one of those possible worlds could be bridged.

The trouble was what happened after you got there. It amounted to living by one's wits; for once the jump across space-time had been made, and you were in the new environment, the conditions of the surroundings had to be accepted completely. It was no good trying to fire a revolver or scratch a match or light a flashlight in the world of Norse myth; these things did not form part of the surrounding mental pattern, and remained obstinately inert masses of useless material. On the other hand, magic . . .

The mist thickened and whirled. Shea felt the pull of Belphebe's hand, clutching his desperately as though something were trying to pull her in the other direction.

Another jerk at Shea's hand reminded him that they might not even wind up in the same place, given that their various mental backgrounds would spread the influence of the generalised spells across different space-time patterns. 'Hold on!' he cried, and clutched Belphebe's hand tighter still.

Shea felt earth under his feet and something hitting him on the head. He realised that he was standing in pouring rain, coming down vertically and with such intensity that he could not see more than a few yards in any direction. His first glance was towards Belphebe; she swung herself into his arms and they kissed damply.

'At least,' she said, disengaging herself a little, 'you are with me, my most dear lord, and so there's nought to fear.'

They looked around, water running off their noses and chins. Shea's heavy woollen shirt was already so soaked that it stuck to his skin, and Belphebe's neat hair was taking on a drowned-rat appearance. She pointed and cried, 'There's one!'

Shea peered towards a lumpish dark mass that had a shape vaguely resembling Pete Brodsky.

'Shea?' came a call, and without waiting for a reply the lump started towards them. As it did so, the downpour lessened and the light brightened.

'Curse it, Shea!' said Brodsky, as he approached. 'What kind of a box is this? If I couldn't work my own racket better, I'd turn myself in for mopery. Where the hell are we?'

'Ohio, I hope,' said Shea. 'And look, shamus, we're better off than we were, ain't we? I'm sorry about this rain, but I didn't order it.'

'All I got to say is you better be right,' said Brodsky gloomily. 'You can get it all for putting the snatch on an officer, and I ain't sure I can square the rap even now. Where's the other guy?'

Shea looked around. 'Walter may be here, but it looks as though he didn't come through to the same place. And if you ask me, the question is not where we are but when we are. It wouldn't do us much good to be back in Ohio in 700 AD, which is about the time we left. If this rain would only let up . . .'

With surprising abruptness the rain did, walking away

in a wall of small but intense downpours. Spots and bars of sky appeared among the clouds wafted along by a brisk steady current of air that penetrated Shea's wet shirt chillingly, and the sun shot an occasional beam through the clouds to touch up the landscape.

It was a good landscape. Shea and his companions were standing in deep grass, on one of the higher spots of an extent of rolling ground. This stretch in turn appeared to be the top of a plateau, falling away to the right. Mossy boulders shouldered up through the grass, which here and there gave way to patches of purple-flowered heather, while daisies nodded in the steady breeze. Here and there was a single tree, but down in the valley beyond their plateau the low land was covered with what appeared at this distance to be birch and oak. In the distance, as they turned to contemplate the scene, rose the heads of far blue mountains.

The cloud-cover thinned rapidly and broke some more. The air had cleared enough so they could now see two other little storms sweeping across the middle distance, trailing their veils of rain. As the patches of sunlight whisked past, the landscape blazed with a singularly vivid green, quite unlike that of Ohio.

Brodsky was the first to speak. 'If this is Ohio, I'm a peterman,' he said. 'Listen, Shea, do I got to tell you again you ain't got much time? If those yaps from the DA's office get started on this, you might just as well hit yourself on the head and save them the trouble. He's coming up for election this fall and needs a nice fat case. And there's the FBI Rover boys – they just love snatch cases, and you can't put no fix in with them that will stick. So you better get me back before people start asking questions.'

Shea said, rather desperately, 'Pete, I'm doing all I can. Honest. I haven't the least idea where we are, or in what period. Until I do, I don't dare try sending us anywhere else. We've already picked up a rather high charge of magical static coming here, and any spell I used without knowing what kind of magic they use around here is apt to make us simply disappear or end up in Hell – you know, real red hell with flames all around, like in a fundamentalist church.'

'Okay,' said Brodsky. 'You got the office. Me, I don't think you got more than a week to get us back at the outside.'

Belphebe pointed, 'Marry, are those not sheep?'

Shea shaded his eyes. 'Right you are, darling,' he said. The objects looked like a collection of lice on a piece of green baize, but he trusted his wife's phenomenal eyesight.

'Sheep,' said Brodsky. One could almost hear the gears grind in his brain as he looked around. 'Sheep.' A beatific expression spread over his face. 'Shea, you must of done it! Three, two, and out we're in Ireland – and if it is, you can hit me on the head if I ever want to go back.'

Shea followed his eyes. 'It does rather look like it,' he said. 'But when . . .'

Something went past with a rush of displaced air. It struck a nearby boulder with a terrific crash and burst into fragments that whizzed about like pieces of an artillery shell.

'Duck!' shouted Shea, throwing himself flat and dragging Belphebe down with him.

Brodsky went into a crouch, lips drawn tight over his teeth, looking around with quick, jerky motions for the source of the missile. Nothing more happened. After a minute, Shea and Belphebe got up and went over to examine a twenty-pound hunk of sandy conglomerate.

Shea said, 'Somebody is chucking hundred-pound boulders around. This may be Ireland, but I hope it isn't the time of Finn McCool or Strongbow.'

'Cripes,' said Brodsky, 'and me without my heater. And you a shiv man with no shiv.'

It occurred to Shea that at whatever period they had hit this place, he *was* in a singularly weaponless state. He climbed on the boulder against which the missile had destroyed itself and looked in all directions. There was no sign of life except the distant, tiny sheep – not even a shepherd or a sheep-dog.

He slid down and sat on a ledge of the boulder and considered, the stone feeling hard against his wet back. 'Sweetheart,' he said, addressing Belphebe, 'it seems to me that whenever we are, the first thing we have to do is find people and get oriented. You're the guide. Which direction's the most likely?'

The girl shrugged. 'My woodcraft is nought without trees,' she said, 'but if you put it so, I'd seek a valley, for people ever live by watercourses.'

'Good idea,' said Shea. 'Let's . . .'

Whizz!

Another boulder flew through the air, but not in their direction. It struck the turf a hundred yards away, bounced clumsily, and rolled out of sight over the hill. Still – no one was visible.

Brodsky emitted a growl, but Belphebe laughed. 'We are encouraged to begone,' she said. 'Come, my lord, let us do no less.'

At that moment another sound made itself audible. It was that of a team of horses and a vehicle whose wheels were in violent need of lubrication. With a drumming of hooves, a jingle of harness, and a squealing of wheels, a chariot rattled up the slope and into view. It was drawn by two huge horses, one grey and one black. The chariot itself was built more on the lines of sulky than those of the open-backed Graeco-Roman chariot, with a seat big enough for two or three persons across the back, and the sides cut low in front to allow for entrance. The vehicle was ornamented with nail-heads and other trim in gold, and a pair of scythe-blades jutted from the hubs.

The driver was a tall, thin freckled man, with red hair trailing from under his golden fillet down over his shoulders. He wore a green kilt and over that a deerskin cloak with arm-holes at elbow length.

The chariot sped straight towards Shea and his companions, who dodged away from the scythes round the edge of the boulder. At the last minute the charioteer reined to a walk and shouted, 'Be off with you if you would keep the heads on your shoulders!'

'Why?' asked Shea.

'Because himself has a rage on. It is tearing up trees and casting boulders he is, and a bad hour it will be for anyone who meets him the day.'

'Who is himself?' said Shea, almost at the same time as Brodsky said, 'Who the hell are you?'

The charioteer pulled up with an expression of astonishment on his face. 'I am Laeg mac Riangabra, and who would himself be but Ulster's hound, the glory of Ireland, Cuchulainn the mighty? He is after killing his only son and has worked himself into a rage. *Ara!* It is ruining the countryside he is, and the sight of you Fomorians would make him the wilder.'

The charioteer cracked his whip, and the horses raced off over the hill, the flying clods dappling the sky. In the direction from which he had come, a good-sized sapling with dangling roots rose against the horizon and fell back.

'Come on!' said Shea, grabbing Belphebe's hand and starting down the slope after the chariot.

'Hey!' said Brodsky, tagging after them, 'Come on back and pal up with this ghee. He's the number one hero of Ireland.'

Another rock bounced on the sward and from the distance a kind of howling was audible.

'I've heard of him,' said Shea, 'and if you want to, we can drop in on him later, but I think that right now is a poor time for calls. He isn't in a pally mood.'

Belphebe said, 'You name him hero, and yet you say he has slain his own son. How can this be?'

Brodsky said, 'It was a bum rap. This Cuchulainn got his girlfriend Aoife pregnant way back when and then gave her the air, see? So she's sore at him, see? So when the kid grows up, she sends him to Cuchulainn under a geas . . .'

'A moment,' said Belphebe. 'What would this geas be?'

'A taboo,' said Shea.

Brodsky said, 'It's a hell of a lot more than that. You

got one these geasa on you and you can't do the thing it's against even if it was to save you from the hot seat. So like I was saying this young ghee, his name is Conla, but he has this geas on him not to tell his name or that of his father to anyone. So when Aoife sends him to Cuchulainn, the big shot challenges the kid and then knocks him off. It ain't good.'

'A tale to mourn, indeed,' said Belphebe. 'How are you so wise in these matters, Master Pete? Are you of this race?'

'I only wisht I was,' said Brodsky fervently. 'It would do me a lot of good on the force. But I ain't, so I dope it this way, see? I'll study this Irish stuff till I know more about it than nobody. And then I got innarested, see?'

They were well down the slope now, the grass dragging at their feet, approaching the impassive sheep.

Belphebe said, 'I trust we shall come soon to where there are people. My bones protest I have not dined.'

'Listen,' said Brodsky, 'This is Ireland, the best country in the world. If you want to feed your face, just knock off one of them sheep. It's on the house. They run the pitch that way.'

'We have neither knife nor fire,' said Belphebe.

'I think we can make out on the fire deal with the metal we have on us and a piece of flint,' said Shea. 'And if we have a sheep killed and a fire going, I'll bet it won't be long before somebody shows up with a knife to share our supper. Anyway, it's worth a try.'

He walked over to a big tree and picked up a length of dead branch that lay near the base. By standing on it and heaving, he broke it somewhat raggedly in half, handing one end to Brodsky. The resulting cudgels did not look especially efficient, but they could be made to do.

'Now,' said Shea, 'If we hide behind that boulder, Belphebe can circle around and drive the flock towards us.'

'Would you be stealing our sheep now, darlings?' said a deep male voice.

Shea looked around. Out of nowhere, a group of men had appeared, standing on the slope above them. There were five of them, in kilts or trews, with mantles of deerskin or wolfhide fastened around their necks. One of them carried a brassbound club, one a clumsy-looking sword, and the other three, spears.

Before Shea could say anything, the one with the club said, 'The heads of the men will look fine in the hall, now. But I will have the woman first.'

'Run!' cried Shea, and took his own advice. The five ran after them.

Belphebe, being unencumbered, soon took the lead. Shea clung to his club, hating to have nothing to hit back with if he were run down. A glance backward showed that Brodsky had either dropped his or thrown it at the pursuers without effect.

'Shea!' yelled the detective. 'Go on – they got me!'

They had not, as a matter of fact, but it was clear they soon would. Shea paused, turned, snatched up a stone about the size of a baseball, and threw it past Brodsky's head at the pursuers. The spearman-target ducked, and they came on, spreading out in a crescent to surround their prey.

'I – can't – run no more,' panted Brodsky. 'Go on.'

'Like hell,' said Shea. 'We can't go back without you. Let's both take the guy with the club.'

The stones arched through the air simultaneously. The clubman ducked, but not far enough; one missile caught his leather cap and sent him sprawling to the grass.

The others whooped and closed in with the evident intention of skewering and carving, when a terrific racket made everyone pause on tiptoe. Down the slope came the chariot that had passed Shea and his group before. The tall, red-haired charioteer was standing in the front, yelling something like 'Ulluullu' while balancing in the back was a smaller, rather dark man.

The chariot bounded and slewed towards them. Before Shea could take in the whole action, one of the hub-head scythes caught a spearman, shearing off both legs neatly, just below the knee. The man fell, shrieking, and at the same instant the small man drew back his arm and threw a javelin right through the body of another.

'It is himself!' cried one of them, and the survivors turned to run.

The small dark fellow spoke to the charioteer, who pulled up his horses. Cuchulainn leaped down from the vehicle, took a sling from his belt and whirled it around his head. The stone struck one of the men in the back of the neck, and down he went. As the man fell, Cuchulainn wound up a second time. Shea thought this one would miss for sure, as the man was now a hundred yards away and going farther fast. But the missile hit him in the head, and he pitched on his face.

'Get out the head bag and fetch me the trophies, dear,' said Cuchulainn.

Ten

Laeg rummaged in the rear of the chariot and produced a large bag and a heavy sword, with which he went calmly to work. Belphebe had turned back, as the rescuer came towards the three. Shea saw a smallish man with curly black hair, not older than himself; heavy black eyebrows and only a faint fuzz on his cheeks to compare with the heavy beards of the defunct five. He was not only an extremely handsome man; there was also a powerful play of musculature under his loose outer garment. The hero's face bore an expression of settled and brooding melancholy, and he was dressed in a long-sleeved white cloak embroidered with gold thread, over a red tunic.

'Thanks a lot,' said Shea. 'You just saved our lives, in case you wondered. How did you happen along?'

' 'Twas Laeg came to me with a tale of three strangers, who might be Fomorians by the look to them, and they were like to be set on by the Lagenians. Now I will be fighting any man in Ireland that gives me the time, but unless you are a hero it is not good to fight at five to two, and it is time that these pigs of Lagenians learned their manners. So now it is time for you to be telling me who you are and where you come from and whither bound. If you are indeed Fomorians, the better for you – King Conchobar is friends with them this year, or I might be making you by the head shorter.'

Shea searched his mind for details of the culture-pattern of the men of Cuchulainn's Ireland. A slip at the beginning might result in their heads being added to the collection bumping each other in Laeg's bag like so many cantaloupes. Brodsky beat him to the punch.

'Jeepers!' he said, in a tone which carried its own message. 'Imagine holding heavy with a zinger like you! I'm Pete Brodsky – give a toss to my friends here, Harold

Shea and his wife Belphebe.' He stuck out his hand.

'We do not come from Fomoria, but from America, an island beyond their land,' said Shea.

Cuchulainn acknowledged the introduction to Shea with a stately nod of courtesy. His eyes swept over Brodsky, and he ignored the out-thrust hand. He addressed Shea. 'Why do you travel in company with such a mountain of ugliness, dear?'

Out of the corner of his eye, Shea could see the cop's wattles swell dangerously. He said hastily; 'He may be no beauty, but he's useful. He's our slave and bodyguard, a good fighting man. Shut up, Pete!'

Brodsky had sense enough to do so. Cuchulainn accepted the explanation with the same sad courtesy and gestured towards the chariot. 'You will be mounting up in the back of my car, and I will drive you to my camp, where there will be an eating before you set out on your journey again.'

He climbed to the front of the chariot himself, while the three wanderers clambered wordlessly to the back seat and held on. Laeg, having disposed of the head bag, touched the horses with a golden goad. Off they went. Shea found the ride a monstrously rough one, for the vehicle had no springs and the road was distinguished by its absence, but Cuchulainn lounged in the seat, apparently at ease.

Presently there loomed ahead a small patch of woods at the bottom of a valley. Smoke rose from a fire. The sun had decided to resolve the question of what time of day it was by setting, so that the hollow lay in shadow. A score or more of men, rough and wild-looking, got to their feet and cheered as the chariot swept into the camp. At the centre of it a huge iron pot bubbled over the fire, and in the background a shelter of poles, slabs of bark and branches had been erected. Laeg pulled up the chariot and lifted the head bag with its lumpish trophies, and there was more cheering.

Cuchulainn sprang down lightly, acknowledged the greeting with a casual wave, then swung to Shea. 'Mac Shea, I am thinking that you are of quality, and as you are not altogether the ugliest couple in the world, you will be eating with me.' He waved an arm. 'Bring the food, darlings.'

Cuchulainn's henchmen busied themselves, with a vast amount of shouting, and running about in patterns that would have made good cat's cradles. One picked up a stool and carried it across the clearing, a second immediately picked it up again and took it back to where it had been.

'Do you think they'll ever get around to feeding us?' said Belphebe in a low tone. But Cuchulainn merely looked on with a slight smile, seeming to regard the performance as somehow a compliment to himself.

After an interminable amount of coming and going, the stool was finally established in front of the lean-to. Cuchulainn sat down on it and with a wave of his hand, indicated that the Sheas were to sit on the ground in front of him. The charioteer Laeg joined them on the ground, which was still decidedly damp after the rain. But, as their clothes had not dried, it didn't seem to matter.

A man brought a large wooden platter on which were heaped the champion's victuals, consisting of a huge cut of boiled pork, a mass of bread, and a whole salmon. Cuchulainn laid it on his knees and set to work on it with fingers and his dagger, saying with a ghost of a smile, 'Now according to the custom of Ireland, Mac Shea, you may challenge the champion for his portion. A man of your inches should be a blithe swordsman, and I have never fought with an American.'

'Thanks,' said Shea, 'but I don't think I could eat that much, anyway, and there's a – what do you call it? – a geas against my fighting anyone who has done something for me, so I couldn't after the way you saved us.' He addressed himself to the slab of bread on which had been placed a pork chop and a piece of salmon, then glanced at Belphebe and added, 'Would it be too much trouble to ask for the loan of a pair of knives? We left in rather a hurry and without our tools.'

A shadow flitted across the face of Cuchulainn. 'It is not well for a man of his hands to be without his weapons. Are you sure, now, that they were not taken away from you?'

Belphebe said, 'We came here on a magical spell, and as you doubtless know, there are some that cannot be spelled in the presence of cold iron.'

'And what could be truer?' agreed Cuchulainn. He clapped his hands and called, 'Bring two knives, darlings. The iron knives, not the bronze.' He chewed, looking at Belphebe. 'And where would you be journeying to, darlings?'

Shea said, 'Back to America, I suppose. We sort of – dropped in to see the greatest hero in Ireland.'

Cuchulainn appeared to take the compliment as a matter of course. 'You come at a poor time. The expedition is over, and now I am going home to sit quietly with my wife Emer, so there will be no fighting.'

Laeg looked up with his mouth full and said, 'You will be quiet if Meddling Maev and Ailill will let you, Cucuc. Some devilment they will be getting up, or it is not the son of Riangabra I am.'

'When my time comes to be killed by the Conachta, then I will be killed by the men of Conacht,' said Cuchulainn, composedly. He was still looking at Belphebe.

Belphebe asked, 'Who stands at the head of the magical art here?'

Cuchulainn said, 'It is true that you said you have a taste for magic. None is greater, nor will be, than Ulster's Cathbadh, adviser to King Conchobar. And now you will come with me to Muirthemne in the morning, rest and fit yourselves, and we will go to Emain Macha to see him together.'

He laid aside his platter and took another look at Belphebe. The little man was as good with a trencher as he was with a sling; there was practically nothing left, and he had had twice as much as Shea.

'That's extremely kind of you,' said Shea. 'Very kind indeed.' It was so very kind that he felt a twinge of suspicion.

'It is not,' said Cuchulainn. 'For those with the gift of beauty, it is no more than their due that they should receive all courtesy.'

He was still looking at Belphebe, who glanced up at the darkening sky. 'My lord,' she said, 'I am somewhat foredone. Would it not be well to seek our rest?'

Shea said, 'It's an idea. Where do we sleep?'

Cuchulainn waved a hand towards the grove. 'Where you will, darlings. No one will disturb you in the camp of Cuchulainn.' He clapped his hands. 'Gather moss for the bed of my friends.'

When they were alone, Belphebe said in a low voice: 'I like not the manner of his approach, though he has done us great good. Cannot you use your art to transport us back to Ohio?'

Shea said, 'I'll take a chance on trying to work out the sorites in the morning. Remember, it won't do us any good to get back alone. We've got to take Pete, or we'll be up on a charge of kidnapping or murdering him, and I don't want to go prowling through this place at night looking for him. Besides, we need light to make the passes.'

Early as they rose, the camp was already astir about them and a fire lighted. As Shea and Belphebe wandered through the camp, looking for Brodsky, they noted it was strangely silent, the elaborate confusion of the previous evening being carried on in whispers or dumb show. Shea grabbed the arm of a bewhiskered desperado hurrying past with a bag of something to inquire the reason.

The man bent close and said in a fierce whisper, 'Sure, 'tis that himself is in his sad mood, and keeping his booth. If you would lose your head, it would be just as well to make a noise.'

'There's Pete,' said Belphebe.

The detective waved a hand and came towards them

from under the trees. He had somehow acquired one of the deerskin cloaks, which was held under his chin with a brass brooch, and he looked unexpectedly cheerful.

'What's the office?' he asked in the same stage whisper the others were using as he approached, them.

'Come with us,' said Shea. 'We're going to try to get back to Ohio. Where'd you get the new clothes?'

'Aw, one of these muzzlers thought he could wrestle, so I slipped him a little jujitsu and won it. Listen, Shea, I changed my mind. I ain't going back. This is the real McCoy.'

'But we want to go back,' said Belphebe, 'and you told us just yesterday that if we showed up without you, our fate would be less than pleasant.'

'Listen, give it a rest. I'm on the legit here, and with that magical stuff of yours, you could be, too. At least I want to stay for the big blow.'

'Come this way,' said Shea, leading away from the centre of the camp to where there was less danger of their voices causing trouble. 'What do you mean by the big blow?'

'From what I got,' said Pete, 'I figured out when we landed. This Maev and Ailill are rustling out the mob and heeling them up to give Cuchulainn a bang on the head. They got all the cousins of people he's bumped off in on the caper, and they're going to put a geas on him that will make him go up against them all at once, and then boom. I want to stay for the payoff.'

'Look here,' said Shea, 'you said only yesterday that we had to get you back within a week. Remember? It was something about your probably being seen going into our house and not coming out.'

'Sure, sure. And if we go back, I'll alibi you. But what for? I'm teaching these guys to wrestle, and what with your magic, maybe you could even take the geas off the big shot and he wouldn't get shoved over.'

'Perhaps I could at that,' said Shea. 'It seems to amount to a kind of psychological compulsion by magical means, and between psychology and magic, I ought to make it.

But no – it's too risky. I daren't take the chance with him making eyes at Belphebe.'

They had emerged from the clump of trees and were at the edge of the slope, with the early sun just touching the tops of the branches above them. Shea went on, 'I'm sorry, Pete, but Belphebe and I don't want to spend the rest of our lives here, and if we're going, we've got to go now. As you said. Now, you two hold hands. Give me your other hand, Belphebe.'

Brodsky obeyed with a somewhat sullen expression. Shea closed his eyes, and began: 'If either A or (B or C) is true, and C or D is false . . .' motioning with his free hand to the end of the sorites.

He opened his eyes again. They were still at the edge of a clump of trees, on a hill in Ireland, watching the smoke from the fire as it rose above the trees to catch the sunshine.

Belphebe asked, 'What's amiss?'

'I don't *know*,' said Shea desperately. 'If I only had something to write with, so I could check over the steps . . . No, wait a minute. Making this work depends on a radical alteration of sense impressions in accordance with the rules of symbolic logic and magic. Now we know that magic works here, so that can't be the trouble. But for symbolic logic to be effective, you have to submit to its effects – that is, be willing. Pete, you're the villain of the piece. You don't want to go back.'

'Don't put the squeeze on me,' said Brodsky. 'I'll play ball.'

'All right. Now I want you to remember that you're going back to Ohio, and that you have a good job there and like it. Besides, you were sent out to find us, and you did. Okay?'

They joined hands again and Shea, constricting his brow with effort, ran through the sorites again, this time altering one or two of the terms to give greater energy. As he reached the end, time seemed to stand still for a second; then *crash!* and a flash of vivid blue lightning struck the tree nearest them, splitting it from top to bottom.

Belphebe gave a little squeal, and a chorus of excited voices rose from the camp.

Shea gazed at the fragments of the splintered tree and said soberly, 'I think that shot was meant for us, and that just about tears it, darling. Pete, you get your wish. We're going to have to stay here at least until I know more about the laws controlling magic in this continuum.'

Two or three of Cuchulainn's men burst excitedly through the trees and came towards them, spears ready. 'It is all right that you are?' one of them called.

'Just practising a little magic,' said Shea, easily. 'Come on, let's go back and join the others.'

In the clearing voices were no longer quenched, and the confusion had become worse than ever. Cuchulainn stood watching the loading of the chariot, with a lofty and detached air. As the three travellers approached he said, 'Now it is to you I am grateful, Mac Shea, with your magical spell for reminding me that things are better done at home than abroad. It is leaving at once we are.'

'Hey!' said Brodsky. 'I ain't had no breakfast.'

The hero regarded him with distaste. 'You will be telling me that I should postpone the journey for the condition of a slave's belly?' he said, and turning to Shea and Belphebe, 'We can eat as we go.'

The ride was smoother than the one of the previous day only because the horses went at a walk so as not to outdistance the column of retainers on foot. Conversation over the squeaking of the wheels began by being sparse and rather boring, with Cuchulainn keeping his chin well down on his chest. But he apparently liked Belphebe's comments on the beauty of the landscape. As it came on to noon he began to chatter, addressing her with an exclusiveness that Shea found disturbing, though he had to admit that the little man talked well, and always with the most perfect courtesy.

The country around them got lower and flatter and flatter and lower, until from the tops of the few rises Shea glimpsed a sharp line of grey-blue across the horizon; the sea. A shower came down and temporarily soaked the column, but nobody paid it much attention, and in the clear sunlit air that followed everyone was soon dry. Cultivation became more common, though there was still less of it than pasturage. Occasionally a lumpish-looking serf, clad in a length of ragged sacking-like cloth wrapped around his middle and a thick veneer of dirt, left off his labours to stare at the band and wave a languid greeting.

At last, over the manes of the horses, Shea saw that they were approaching a stronghold. This consisted of a stockade of logs with a huge double gate.

Belphebe surveyed it critically and whispered behind her hand to Shea, 'It could be taken with fire-arrows.'

'I don't think they have many archers or very good ones,' he whispered back. 'Maybe you can show them something.'

The gate was pushed open creakingly by more bearded warriors, who shouted: 'Good-day to you, Cucuc! Good luck to Ulster's hound!'

The gate was wide enough to admit the chariot, scythe-blades and all. As the vehicle rumbled through the opening, Shea glimpsed houses of various shapes and sizes, some of them evidently stables and barns. The biggest of all was the hall in the middle, whose heavily thatched roof came down almost to the ground at the sides.

Laeg pulled up. Cuchulainn jumped down, waved his hand, and cried, 'Muirthemne welcomes you, Americans!' All the others applauded as though he had said something particularly brilliant.

He turned to speak to a fat man, rather better dressed than the rest, when another man came out of the main hall and walked rapidly towards them. The newcomer was a thin man of medium height, elderly but vigorous, slightly bent and carrying a stick, on which he leaned now and again. He had a long white beard, and a purple robe covered him from neck to ankle.

'The best of the day to you, Cathbadh,' said Cuchulainn. 'This is surely a happy hour that brings you here, but where is my darling Emer?'

'Emer has gone to Emain Macha,' said Cathbadh. 'Conchobar summoned her . . .'

'Ara!' shouted Cuchulainn. 'Is it a serf that I am, that the King can send for my wife every time he takes it into the head of him? He is . . .'

'It is not that at all, at all,' said Cathbadh. 'He summons you, too, and for that he sent me instead of Levarcham, for he knows you might not heed her word if you took it into that wilful head of yours to disobey, whereas it is myself can put a geas on you to go.'

'And why does himself want us at Emain Macha?'

'Would I be knowing all the secrets in the heart of a King?'

Shea asked, 'Are you the court druid?'

Cathbadh became aware of him for the first time, and Cuchulainn made introductions. Shea explained, 'It seems to me that the King might want you at the court for your own protection, so the druids can keep Maev's sorcerers from putting a spell on you. That's what she's going to do.'

'How do you know of this?' asked Cathbadh.

'Through Pete here. He sometimes knows about things that are going to happen before they actually take place. In our country we call it second sight.'

Cuchulainn wrinkled his nose. 'That ugly slave?'

'Yeh, me,' said Brodsky, who had approached the group. 'And you better watch your step, handsome, because somebody's going to hang you up to dry unless you do something about it.'

'If it is destined none can alter it,' said Cuchulainn. 'Fergus! Have the bath water heated.' He turned to Shea. 'Once you are properly washed and garbed you will look well enough for the board in my beautiful house. I will lend you some proper garments, for I cannot bear the sight of those Fomorian-like rags.'

Eleven

Along the side of the main hall was an alcove made of screens of wattle, set at an angle that provided privacy for those within. In the alcove stood Cuchulainn's bathtub, a large and elaborate affair of bronze. A procession of the women of the manor were now coming in from the well with jugs of water, which they emptied into the tub. Meanwhile the men were poking up the fire at the end of the hall and adding a number of stones of about five to ten pounds' weight.

Brodsky sidled up to Shea, as they stood in the half-light, orienting themselves. 'Listen, I don't want to blow the whistle on a bum rap, but you better watch it. The racket they have here, this guy can make a pass at Belphebe in his own house, and it's legit. You ain't got no beef coming.'

'I was afraid of that,' said Shea, unhappily. 'Look there.'

'There' was a row of wooden spikes projecting from one of the horizontal strings along the wall, and most of these spikes were occupied by human heads. As they watched Laeg brought in the head bag and added the latest trophies to the collection, pressing them down firmly. Some of those already in place were quite fresh, while others had been there so long that there was little left of them but a skull with a little hair adhering to the scalp.

'Jeepers!' said Brodsky, 'and if you start beefing, he'll put you there, too. Give me time – I'll try to think of some way to rumble his line.'

'Make way!' shouted a huge bewhiskered retainer. The three dodged as the man ran past them, carrying a large stone, smoking from the fire, in a pair of tongs. The man dashed into the alcove. There was a splash and a loud hiss. Another retainer followed with a second stone while the first was on his return trip. In a few minutes all the stones had been transferred to the bathtub. Shea looked around the screen and saw that the water was steaming gently.

Cuchulainn sauntered past into the bathroom and tested the water with an inquisitive finger. 'That will do, dears.'

The retainers picked the stones out of the water with their tongs and piled them in the corner, then went around from behind the screen. Cuchulainn reached up to pull off his tunic, then saw Shea.

'I am going to undress for the bath,' he said. 'Surely, you would not be wanting to remain here, now.'

Shea turned back into the main room just in time to see Brodsky smack one fist into the other palm. 'Got it!'

'Got what?' said Shea.

'How to needle this hot tomato.' He looked around, then pulled Shea and Belphebe closer. 'Listen, the big shot putting the scram on you now just reminded me. The minute he makes a serious pass at you, Belle, you gotta go into a strip-tease act. In public, where everybody can get a gander at it.'

Belphebe gasped. Shea asked. 'Are you out of your head? That sounds to me like trying to put a fire out with gasoline.'

'I tell you he can't take it!' Brodsky's voice was low but urgent. 'They can't none of them. One time when this guy was going to put the slug on everyone at the court, the King sent out a bunch of babes with bare knockers, and they nearly had to pick him up in a basket.'

'I like this not,' said Belphebe, but Shea said, 'A nudity taboo! That could be part of a culture pattern, all right. Do they all have it?'

'Yeah, and but good,' said Brodsky. 'They even croak of it. What gave me the tip was him putting the chill on you before he started to undress – he was doing you a favour.'

Cuchulainn stepped out of the alcove, buckling a belt around a fresh tunic, emerald-green with embroidery of golden thread. He scrubbed his long hair with a towel and ran a comb through it, while Laeg took his place behind the screen.

Belphebe said, 'Is there to be but one water for all?'

Cuchulainn said, 'There is plenty of soapwort. Cleanliness is good for beauty.' He glanced at Brodsky. 'The slave can bathe in the trough outside.'

'Listen . . .' began Brodsky, but Shea put a hand on his arm, and to cover up, asked, 'Do your druids use spells of transportation – from one place to another?'

'There is little a good druid cannot do – but I would advise you not to use the spells of Cathbadh unless you are a hero as well as a maker of magic, for they are very mighty.'

He turned to watch the preparations for dinner with a sombre satisfaction. Laeg presently appeared, his toilet made, and from another direction one of the women brought garments which she took into the bathroom for Shea and Belphebe. Shea started to follow his wife, but remembered what Brodsky had said about the taboo, and decided not to take a chance on shocking his hosts. She came out soon enough in a floor-length gown that clung to her all over, and he noted with displeasure that it was the same green and embroidered pattern as Cuchulainn's tunic.

After Shea had dealt with water almost cold and a towel already damp, his own costume turned out to be a saffron tunic and tight knitted scarlet trews which he imagined as looking quite effective.

Belphebe was watching the women around the fire. Over in the shadows under the eaves sat Pete Brodsky, cleaning his fingernails with a bronze knife, a chunky, middle-aged man – a good hand in a fight, with his knowledge of jujitsu and his quick reflexes, and not a bad companion. Things would be a lot easier, though, if he hadn't fouled up the spell by wanting to stay where he was. Or had that been responsible?

Old Cathbadh came stumping up with his stick. 'Mac Shea,' he said, 'the Little Hound is after telling me that you also are a druid, who came here by magical arts from a distant place, and can summon lightning from the skies.'

'It's true enough,' said Shea. 'Doubtless you know those spells.'

'Doubtless I do,' said Cathbadh, looking sly. 'We must hold converse on matters of our craft. We will be teaching each other some new spells, I am thinking.'

Shea frowned. The only spell he was really interested in was one that would take Belphebe and himself – and Pete – back to Garaden, Ohio, and Cathbadh probably didn't know that one. It would be a question of getting at the basic assumptions, and more or less working out his own method of putting them to use.

Aloud he said, 'I think we can be quite useful to each other. In America, where I come from, we have worked out some of the general principles of magic, so that it is only necessary to learn the procedures in various places.'

Cathbadh shook his head. 'You do be telling me – and it is the word of a druid, so I must believe you – but 'tis hard to credit that a druid could travel among the Scythians of Greece or the Scots of Egypt, with all the strange gods they do be having, and still be protected by his spells as well as at home.'

Shea got a picture of violently confused geography. But then, he reflected, the correspondence between this world and his own would only be rough, anyway. There might be Scots in Egypt here.

Just then Cuchulainn came out of his private room and sat down without ceremony at the head of the table. The others gathered round. Laeg took the place at one side of the hero and Cathbadh at the other. Shea and Belphebe were nodded to the next places, opposite each other. A good-looking serf woman with hair bound back from her forehead filled a large golden goblet at Cuchulainn's place with wine from a golden ewer, then smaller silver cups at the places of Laeg and Cathbadh, and copper mugs for Shea and Belphebe. Down the table the rest of the company had leather jacks and barley beer.

Cuchulainn said to Cathbadh, 'Will you make the

sacrifice, dear?'

The druid stood up, spilled a few drops on the floor and chanted to the gods Bile, Danu, and Ler. Shea decided that it was only imagination that he was hearing the sound of beating wings, and only the approach of the meal that gave him a powerful sense of internal comfort, but there was no doubt that Cathbadh knew his stuff.

He knew it, too. 'Was that not fine, now?' he said, as he sat down next to Shea. 'Can you show me anything in your outland magic ever so good?'

Scea thought. It wouldn't do any harm to give the old codger a small piece of sympathetic magic, and might help his own reputation. He said, 'Move your wine-cup over next to mine, and then watch it carefully.'

There would have to be a spell to link the two if he were going to make Cathbadh's wine disappear as he drank his own, and the only one he could think of at the moment was the 'Double, double' from 'Macbeth.' He murmured that under his breath, making the hand passes he had learned in Faerie.

Then he said, 'Now, watch,' picked up his mug and set it to his lips.

Whoosh!

Out of Cathbadh's cup a geyser of wine leaped as though driven by a pressure hose, nearly reaching the ceiling before it broke up to descend in a rain of glittering drops, while the guests at the head of the table leaped to their feet to draw back from the phenomenon. Cathbadh was a fast worker; he lifted his stick and struck the hurrying stream of liquid, crying something unintelligible in a high voice. Abruptly the gusher was quenched and there was only the table, swimming with wine, and serf women rushing to mop up the mess.

Cuchulainn said, 'This is a very beautiful piece of magic, Mac Shea, and it is a pleasure to have so notable a druid among us. But you would not be making fun of us, would you?' He looked dangerous.

'Not me,' said Shea, 'I only . . .'

Whatever he intended to say was cut off by a sudden

burst of unearthly howling from somewhere outside. Shea glanced around rather wildly, feeling that things were getting out of hand. Cuchulainn said, 'You need not be minding that at all, now. It will only be Uath, and because the moon has reached her term.'

'I don't understand,' said Shea.

'The women of Ulster were not good enough for Uath, so he must be going to Connacht and courting the daughter of Ollgaeth the druid. This Ollgaeth is no very polite man; he said no Ultonian should have his daughter, and when Uath persisted, he put a geas on Uath that when the moon fills he must howl the night out, and a geas on his own daughter that she cannot abide the sound of howling. I am thinking that Ollgaeth's head is due for a place of honour.' He looked significantly at his collection.

Shea said, 'But I still don't understand. If you can put a geas on someone, can't it be taken off again?'

Cuchulainn looked mournful, Cathbadh embarrassed, and Laeg laughed. 'Now you will be making Cathbadh sad, and our dear Cucuc is too polite to tell you, but the fact is no other than that Ollgaeth is so good a druid that no one can lift the spells he lays, nor lay one he cannot lift.'

Outside, Uath's mournful howl rose again. Cuchulainn said to Belphebe, 'Does he trouble you, dear? I can have him removed, or the upper part of him.'

As the meal progressed, Shea noticed that Cuchulainn was putting away an astonishing quantity of the wine, talking almost exclusively with Belphebe, although the drink did not seem to have much effect on the hero but to intensify his sombre courtesy. But, when the table was cleared, he lifted his goblet to drain it, looked at Belphebe from across the table, and nodded significantly.

Shea got up and ran around the table to place a hand on her shoulder. Out of the corner of his eye, he saw Pete Brodsky getting up, too. Cuchulainn's face bore the faintest of smiles. 'It is sorry to discommode you I am,' he said, 'but this is by the rules and not even a challenging matter. So now, Belphebe, darling, you will just come to my room.'

He got up and started towards Belphebe, who got up, too, backing away. Shea tried to keep between them and racked his brain hopelessly for some kind of spell that might stop this business. Everyone else was standing up and pushing to watch the little drama.

Cuchulainn said, 'Now you would not be getting in my way, would you, Mac Shea, darling?' His voice was gentle, but there was something incredibly ferocious in the way he uttered the words, and Shea suddenly realised he was facing a man who had a sword. Outside, Uath howled mournfully.

Beside him, Belphebe herself suddenly leaped for one of the weapons hanging on the wall and tugged, but in vain. It had been so securely fastened with staples that it would have taken a pry bar to get it loose. Cuchulainn laughed.

Behind and to the left of Shea, Brodsky's voice rose, 'Belle, you stiff, do like I told you!'

She turned back as Cuchulainn drew nearer and with set face crossed her arms and whipped the green gown off over her head. She stood in her underwear.

There was a simultaneous gasp and groan of horror from the audience. Cuchulainn stopped, his mouth coming open.

'Go on!' yelled Brodsky in the background. 'Give it the business!'

Belphebe reached behind her to unhook her brassiere. Cuchulainn staggered as though he had been struck. He threw one arm across his eyes, reached the table and brought his face down on it, pounding the wood with the other fist.

'*Ara!*' he shouted. 'Take her away! Is it killing me you will be and in my own hall, and me your host that has saved your life?'

'Will you let her alone?' asked Shea.

'I will that for the night.'

'Mac Shea, take his offer,' advised Laeg from the head

of the table. He looked rather greenish himself. 'If his rage comes on him, none of us will be safe.'

'Okay. Honest,' said Shea and held Belphebe's dress for her.

There was a universal sigh of relief from the background. Cuchulainn staggered to his feet. 'It is not feeling well that I am, darlings,' he said, and picking up the golden ewer of wine, made for his room.

Twelve

There was a good deal of excited gabble among the retainers as Belphebe walked back to her place without looking to right or left, but they made room for Shea and Brodsky to join her. The druid looked shrewdly at the closed door and said, 'If the Little Hound drinks too much by himself, he may be brooding on the wrong you are after doing him, and a sad day that would be. If he comes out with the hero-light playing round his head, run for your lives.'

Belphebe said, 'But where would we go?'

'Back to your own place. Where else?'

Shea frowned. 'I'm not sure . . .' he began when Brodsky cut in suddenly, 'Say,' he said, 'your boss ain't really got no right to get bugged up. We had to play it that way.'

Cathbadh swung to him. 'And why, serf?'

'Don't call me serf. She's got a fierce geas on her. Any guy that touches her gets a bellyache and dies of it. Her husband only stands it because he's a magician. It's lucky we put the brakes on before the boss got her in that room, or he'd be ready for the lilies right now.'

Cathbadh's eyebrows shot up like a seagull taking off. 'Himself should know of this,' he said. 'There would be less blood shed in Ireland if more people opened their mouths to explain things before they put their feet in them.'

He got up, went to the bedroom door and knocked. There was a growl from within, Cathbadh entered, and a few minutes later came out with Cuchulainn. The latter's step was visibly unsteady, and his melancholy seemed to have deepened. He walked to the head of the table and sat down in the chair again.

'Sure, and this is the saddest tale in the world I'm

hearing about your wife having such a bad geas on her. The evening is spoilt and all. I hope the black fit does not come on me, for then it will be blood and death I need to restore me.'

There were a couple of gasps audible and Laeg looked alarmed, but Cathbadh said hastily, 'The evening is not so spoilt as you think, Cucuc. This Mac Shea is evidently a very notable druid and spell maker, but I think I am a better. Did you notice how quickly I put down his wine fountain? Would it not lift your heart, now, to see the two of us engage in a contest of magic?'

Cuchulainn clapped his hands. 'Never was truer word spoken. You will just do that, darlings.'

Shea said, 'I'm afraid I can't guarantee . . .' but Belphebe plucked his sleeve and with her head close to his, whispered, 'Do it. There is a danger here.'

'It isn't working right,' Shea whispered back.

Outside rose the mournful sound of Uath's howling. 'Can you not use your psychology on him out there?' the girl asked. 'It will be magic to them.'

'A real psychoanalysis would take days,' said Shea. 'Wait a minute, though – we seem to be in a world where the hysteric type is the norm. That means a high suggestibility, and we might get something out of post-hypnotic suggestion.'

Cuchulainn from the head of the table said, 'It is not all night we have to wait.'

Shea turned round and said aloud, 'How would it be if I took the geas off that character out there training to be a bar-room tenor? I understand that's something Cathbadh hasn't been able to do.'

Cathbadh said, 'If you can do this, it will be a thing worth seeing, but I will not acknowledge you can do it until I have seen it.'

'All right,' said Shea. 'Bring him in.'

'Laeg, dear, go get us Uath,' said Cuchulainn. He took a drink, looked at Belphebe and his expression became morose again.

Shea said, 'Let's see. I want a small bright object. May I

borrow one of your rings, Cuchulainn? That one with the big stone would do nicely.'

Cuchulainn slid the ring down the table as Laeg returned, firmly gripping the arm of a stocky young man, who seemed to be offering some resistance to the process. Just as they got in the door Uath flung back his head and emitted a blood-curdling howl. Laeg dragged him forward, howling away.

Shea turned to the others. 'Now if this magic is going to work, I'll need a little room. Don't come too near us while I'm spinning the spell, or you'll be apt to get caught in it, too.' He arranged a pair of seats well back from the table and attached a thread to the ring.

Laeg pushed Uath into one of the seats. 'That's a bad geas you have there, Uath,' said Shea, 'and I want you to co-operate with me in getting rid of it. You'll do everything I tell you, won't you?'

The man nodded. Shea lifted the ring, said, 'Watch this,' and began twirling the thread back and forth between thumb and forefinger, so that the ring rotated first one way and then the other, sending out a flickering gleam of reflection from the rushlights. Meanwhile Shea talked to Uath in a low voice, saying 'sleep' now and then in the process. Behind him he could hear an occasionally caught breath and could almost feel the atmosphere of suspense.

Uath went rigid.

Shea asked in a low voice, 'Can you hear me, Uath?'

'That I can.'

'You will do what I say.'

'That I will.'

'When you wake up, you won't suffer from this howling geas any more.'

'That I will not.'

'To prove that you mean it, the first thing you do on waking will be to clap Laeg on the shoulder.'

'That I will.'

Shea repeated his directions several times, varying the words, and making Uath repeat them after him. There was no use taking a chance on slip-ups. At last he brought him out of the hypnotic trance with a snap of the fingers and a sharp 'Wake up!'

Uath stared about him with an air of bewilderment. Then he got up, walked over to the table and clapped Laeg on the shoulder. There was an appreciative murmur from the audience.

Shea asked, 'How do you feel, Uath?'

'It is just fine that I am feeling. I do not want to be howling at the moon at all now, and I'm thinking the geas is gone for good. I thank your honour.' He came down the table, seized Shea's hand and kissed it and joined the other retainers at the lower part of the table.

Cathbadh said, 'That is a very good magic, indeed, and not the least of it was the small geas you put on him to lay his hand on Laeg's shoulder at the same time. And true it is that I have been unable to lift this geas. But as one man can run faster, so can another one climb faster, and I will demonstrate by taking the geas off your wife, which you have evidently not been able to deal with.'

'I'm not sure . . .' began Shea, doubtfully.

'Let not youself be worried,' said Cuchulainn. 'It will not harm her at all, and in the future she can be more courteous in the high houses she visits.'

The druid rose and pointed a long, bony finger at Belphebe. He chanted some sort of rhythmic affair which began in a gibberish of unknown language, but became more and more intelligible, ending with: '. . . and by oak, ash and yew, by the beauty of Aengus and the strength of Ler and by authority as high druid of Ulster, let this geas be lifted from you, Belphebe! Let it pass! Out with it! It is erased, cancelled and no more to be heard of!' He tossed up his arms and then sat down. 'How do you feel, darling?'

'In good sooth, not much different than before,' said Belphebe. 'Should I?'

Cuchulainn said, 'But how can we know now that the spell has worked? Aha! I have it! Come with me.' He rose and came round the table, and in response to Shea's exclamation of fury and Belphebe's of dismay, added, 'Only as far as the door. Have I not given you my word?'

He bent over Belphebe, put one arm around her and reached for her hand, then reeled back clutching his stomach with both hands and gasping for breath. Cathbadh and Laeg were on their feet. So was Shea.

Cuchulainn staggered against Laeg's arm, wiped a sleeve across his eyes and said, 'Now the American is the winner, since your removal spell has failed, and it was like to be the death of me that the touch of her was. Do you be trying it yourself, Cathbadh, dear.'

The druid reached out and laid a cautious finger on Belphebe's arm. Nothing happened.

Laeg said, 'Did not the serf say that a magician was proof against this geas?'

Cathbadh said, 'You may have the right of it there, although, but I am thinking myself there is another reason. Cucuc wished to take her to his bed, while I was not thinking of that at all, at all.'

Cuchulainn sat down again and addressed Shea. 'A good thing it is, indeed, that I was protected from the work of this geas. Has it not proved obstinate even to the druids of your own country?'

'Very,' said Shea. 'I wish I could find someone who could deal with it.' He had been more surprised than Cuchulainn by the latter's attack of cramps, but in the interval he had figured it out. Belphebe hadn't had any geas on her in the first place. Therefore, when Cathbadh threw at her a spell designed to lift a geas. it took the opposite effect of laying on her a very good geas indeed. That was elementary magicology, and under the conditions he was rather grateful to Cathbadh.

Cathbadh said, 'In America there may be none to deal with such a matter, but in Ireland there is a man both bold and clever enough to lift the spell.'

'Who's he?' asked Shea.

'That will be Ollgaeth of Cruachan, at the court of Ailill and Maev, who put the geas on Uath.'

Brodsky, from beside Shea spoke up. 'He's the guy that's going to put one on Cuchulainn before the big mob takes him.'

'*Wurra!*' said Cathbadh to Shea. 'Your slave must have a second mind to go with his second sight. The last time he spoke, it would only be a spell that Ollgaeth would be putting on the Little Hound.'

'Listen, punk,' said Brodsky in a tone of exasperation, 'get the stones out of your head. This is the pitch: this Maev and Aillil are mobbing up everybody that owes Cuchulainn here a score, and when they get them all together, they're going to put a geas on him that will make him fight them all at once, and it's too bad.'

Cathbadh combed his beard with his fingers. 'If this be true . . .' he began.

'It's the McCoy. Think I'm on the con?'

'I was going to say that if it be true, it is high tidings from a low source. Nor do I see precisely how it may be dealt with. If it were a matter of spells only . . .'

Cuchulainn said with mournful and slightly alcoholic gravity, 'I would fight them all without the geas, but if I am fated to fall, then that is an end of me.'

Cathbadh turned to Shea. 'You see the trouble we have with himself. Does your second sight reach further, slave?'

Brodsky said, 'Okay, lug, you asked for it. After Cuchulainn gets rubbed out, there'll be a war and practically everybody in the act gets knocked off, including you and Ailill and Maev. How do you like it?'

'As little as I like the look of your face,' said Cathbadh. He addressed Shea. 'Can this foretelling be trusted?'

'I've never known him to be wrong.'

Cathbadh glanced from one to the other till one could almost hear his brains rumbling. Then he said, 'I am thinking, Mac Shea, that you will be having business at Ailill's court.'

'What gives you such an idea?'

'You will be wanting to see Ollgaeth in this matter of your wife's geas, of course. A wife with a geas like that is like one with a bad eye, and you can never be happy until it is removed entirely. You will take your man with you, and he will tell his tale and let Maev know that we know of her schemings, and they will be no more use than trying to feed a boar on bracelets.'

Brodsky snapped his fingers and said, 'Take him up,' in a heavy whisper, but Shea said, 'Look here, I'm not at all sure that I want to go to Ailill's court. Why should I? And if this Maev is as determined as she seems to be, I don't think you'll stop her by telling her you know what she's up to.'

'On the first point,' said the druid, 'there is the matter that Cucuc saved your life and all, and you would be grateful to him, not to mention the geas. And for the second, it is not so much Maev that I would be letting know we see through her planning as Ollgaeth. For he will know as well as yourself, that if we learn of the geas before he lays it, all the druids at Conchobar's court will chant against him, and he will have no more chance of making it bite than a dog does of eating an apple.'

'Mmm,' said Shea. 'Your point about gratitude is a good one, even if I can't quite see the validity of the other. What we want mostly is to get to our own home, though.' He stifled a yawn. 'We can take a night to sleep on it and decide in the morning. Where do we sleep?'

'Finn will show you to a chamber,' said Cuchulainn. 'Myself and Cathbadh will be staying up the while to discuss on this matter of Maev.' He smiled his charming and melancholy smile.

Finn guided the couple to a guest-room at the back of the building, handed Shea a rush-light and closed the door, as Belphebe put up her arms to be kissed.

The next second Shea was doubled up and knocked flat to the floor by a super-edition of the cramps.

Belphebe bent over him. 'Are you hurt, Harold?' she asked.

He pulled himself to a sitting posture with his back against the wall. 'Not – seriously,' he gasped. 'It's that geas. It doesn't take any time out for husbands.'

The girl considered. 'Could you not relieve me of it as you did the one who howled?'

Shea said, 'I can try, but I can pretty well tell in advance that it won't work. Your personality is too tightly integrated – just the opposite of these hysterics around here. That is, I wouldn't stand a chance of hypnotizing you.'

'You might do it by magic.'

Shea scrambled the rest of the way to his feet. 'Not till I know more. Haven't you noticed I've been getting an over-charge – first that stroke of lightning and then the wine fountain? There's something in this continuum that seems to reverse my kind of magic.'

She laughed a little. 'If that's the law, why there's an end. You have but to summon Pete and make a magic that would call for us to stay here, then hey, presto! we are returned.'

'I don't dare take the chance, darling. It might work and it might not – and even if it did, you'd be apt to wind up in Ohio with the geas still on you, and we really would be in trouble. We do take our characteristics along with us when we make the jump. And anyway, I don't know *how* to get back to Ohio yet.'

'What's to be done, then?' the girl said. 'For surely you have a plan, as always.'

'I think the only thing we can do is take up Cathbadh's scheme and go see this Ollgaeth. At least, he ought to be able to get rid of that geas.'

All the same, Shea had to sleep on the floor.

Thirteen

Harold Shea, Belphebe, and Pete Brodsky rode steadily at a walk across the central plain of Ireland, the Sheas on horses, Brodsky on a mule which he sat with some discomfort, leading a second mule carrying the provisions and equipment that Cuchulainn had pressed on them. Their accoutrements included serviceable broadswords at the hips of Shea and Brodsky and a neat dagger at Belphebe's belt. Her request for a bow had brought forth only miserable sticks that pulled no farther than the breast and were quite useless beyond a range of fifty yards, and these she had refused.

All the first day they climbed slowly into the uplands of Monaghan. They followed the winding course of the Erne for some miles and splashed across it at a ford, then struck the boglands of western Cavan. Sometimes there was a road of sorts, sometimes they plodded across grassy moors, following the vague and verbose directions of peasants. As they skirted patches of forest, deer started and ran before them, and once a tongue-lolling wolf trotted parallel to their track for a while before abandoning the game.

By nightfall they had covered at least half their journey. Brodsky, who had begun by feeling sorry for himself, began to recover somewhat under the ministrations of Belphebe's excellent camp cookery, and announced that he had seen quite enough of ancient Ireland and was ready to go back.

'I don't get it,' said he. 'Why don't you just mooch off the way you came here?'

'Because I'm unskilled labour now,' explained Shea. 'You saw Cathbadh make that spell – he started chanting in the archaic language and brought it down to date. I get the picture, but I'd have to learn the archaic. Unless I can get someone else to send us back. And I'm worried about that. As you said, we've got to work fast. What are you going to tell them if they've started looking for you when we get back?'

'Ah, nuts,' said Brodsky. 'I'll level with them. The force is so loused up with harps that are always cutting up touches about how hot Ireland is that they'll give it a play whether they believe me or not.'

Belphebe said in a small voice, 'But I would be at home.'

'I know, kid,' said Shea. 'So would I. If I only knew how.'

Morning showed mountains on the right, with a round peak in the midst of them. The journey went more slowly than on the pervious day, principally because all three had not developed riding callouses. They pulled up that evening at the hut of a peasant rather more prosperous than the rest, and Brodsky more than paid for their food and lodging with tales out of Cetlic lore. The pseudo-Irishman certainly had his uses.

The next day woke in rain, and though the peasant assured them that Rath Cruachan was no more than a couple hours' ride distant, the group became involved in fog and drizzle, so that it was not till afternoon that they skirted Loch Key and came to Magh Ai, the Plain of Livers. The cloaks with which Cuchulainn had furnished them were of fine wool, but all three were soaked and silent by time a group of houses came into sight through air slightly clearing.

There were about as many of the buildings as would constitute an incorporated village in their own universe, surrounded by the usual stockade and wide gate – unmistakably Cruachan of the Poets, the capital of Connacht.

As they approached along an avenue of trees and shrubbery, a boy about thirteen, in shawl and kilt and carrying a miniature spear, popped out of the bushes and cried: 'Stand there! Who is it you are and where are you going?'

It might be important not to smile at this diminutive

warrior. Shea identified himself gravely and asked in turn, 'And who are you, sir?'

'I am Goistan mac Idha, of the boy troop of Cruachan, and it is better not to interfere with me.'

Shea said, 'We have come from a far country to see your King and Queen and the druid Ollgaeth.'

He turned and waved his spear towards where a building like that at Muirthemne, but more ornate, loomed over the stockade, then marched ahead of them down the road.

At the gate of the stockade was a pair of hairy soldiers, but their spears were leaning against the posts and they were too engrossed in a game of knuckle-bones even to look up as the party rode through. The clearing weather seemed to have brought activity to the town. A number of people were moving about, most of whom paused to stare at Brodsky, who had flatly refused to discard the pants of his brown business suit and was evidently not dressed for the occasion.

The big house was built of heavy oak beams and had wooden shingles instead of the usual thatch. Shea stared with interest at windows with real glass in them, even though the panes were little diamond-shaped pieces half the size of a hand and far too irregular to see through.

There was a doorkeeper with a beard badly in need of trimming and lopsided to the right. Shea got off his horse and advanced to him, saying, 'I am Mac Shea, a traveller from beyond the island of the Fomorians, with my wife and bodyguard. May we have an audience with their majesties, and their great druid, Ollgaeth?'

The doorkeeper inspected the party with care and then grinned. 'I am thinking,' he said, 'that your honour will please the Queen with your looks, and your lady will please himself, so you had best go along in. But this ugly lump of a bodyguard will please neither, and as they are very sensitive and this is judgement day, he will no doubt be made a head shorter for the coming, so he had best stay with your mounts.'

Shea glanced round in time to see Brodsky replace his

expression of fury with the carefully cultivated blank that policemen use, and helped Belphebe off her horse.

Inside, the main hall stretched away with the usual swords and spears in the usual places on the wall, and a rack of heads, not as large as Cuchulainn's. In the middle of the hall, surrounded at a respectful distance by retainers and armed soldiers, stood an oaken dais, ornamented with strips of bronze and silver. It held two big carven arm-chairs, in which lounged, rather than sat, the famous sovereigns of Connacht.

Maev might have been in her early forties, still strikingly beautiful, with a long, pale, unlined face, pale blue eyes and yellow hair, hanging in long braids. For a blonde without the aid of cosmetics, she had remarkably red lips.

King Ailill was a less impressive figure than his consort, some inches shorter, fat and paunchy, with small close-set eyes constantly moving and a straggly pepper-and-salt beard. He seemed unable to keep his fingers still. An ulcer type, thought Shea; would be a chain smoker if tobacco existed in this part of the space-time continuum.

A young man in a blue kilt, wearing a silver-hilted shortsword over a tunic embroidered with gold thread, seemed to be acting as usher to make sure that nobody got to the royal couple out of turn. He spotted the new-comers at once, and worked his way towards them.

'Will you be seeking an audience, or have you come merely to look at the greatest King in Ireland?' he asked. His eyes ran appreciatively over Belphebe's contours.

Shea identified himself, adding, 'We have come to pay our respects to the King and Queen . . . ah . . .'

'Maine mac Aililla, Maine mo Epert,' said the young man.

This would be one of the numerous sons of Ailill and Maev, who had all been given the same name. But he stood in their path without moving.

'Can we speak to them?' Shea said.

Maine mo Epert put back his head and looked down an aristocratic nose. 'Since you are foreigners, you are evidently not knowing that it is the custom in Connacht to have a present for the man who brings you before a King. But I will be forgiving your ignorance.' He smiled a charming smile.

Shea glanced at Belphebe and she looked back in dismay. Their total possessions consisted of what they stood in. 'But we have to see them,' he said. 'It may be as important to them as to us.'

Maine mo Epert smiled again.

Shea said, 'How about a nice broadsword?' and pushed forward his hilt.

'I have a better one,' said Maine mo Epert, exasperatingly, and pushed forward his. 'If it were a jewel, now . . .'

'How about seeing Ollgaeth the druid?'

'It is a rule that he will see none but those the Queen sends him.'

Shea felt like whipping out the broadsword and taking a crack at him, but that would probably not be considered polite. Suddenly Belphebe beside him said:

'Jewels have we none, sirrah, but from your glances, there is something you would prize more. I am sure that in accordance with your custom, my husband would be glad to lend me to you for the night.'

Shea gasped, and then remembered. That geas she had acquired could be handy as well as troublesome. But it had better not be taken off till morning.

Maine mo Epert's smile turned into a grin that made Shea want more than ever to swat him, but he clapped his hands and began to push people aside. Shea had just time to whisper, 'Nice work, kid,' when the usher pushed a couple of people from the end of a bench and sat them down in the front row, facing the royal pair. At the moment a couple of spearmen were holding a serf and giving evidence that he had stolen a pork shop.

Maev looked at Ailill, who said, 'Ahem – since the lout was starving, perhaps we ought to exercise mercy and let him off with the loss of a hand.'

'Do not be a fool,' said Maev, 'when it is not necessary at all. What! A man in Connacht of the heroes who is so weak-witted that he must starve? Hang him or burn him, would be my decision if I were king.'

'Very well, darling,' said Ailill. 'Let the man be hung.'

Two little groups stepped forward next, glaring at each other. Maine mo Epert began to introduce them, but before he got half way through, Maev said, 'I know of this case and it promises to be a long one. Before we hear it I would willingly learn something of the business of the handsome pair of strangers you have brought in.'

Maine mo Epert said, 'This is a pair from a distant island called America. The Mac Shea and his wife, Belphebe. They wish to pay their respects.'

'Let him speak,' said Maev.

Shea wondered whether he ought to make an obeisance, but as no one else seemed to be doing it, he merely stepped forward and said, 'Queen, you have become so famous that even in America we have heard of you, and we could not restrain the desire to see you. Also, I would like to see your famous druid, Ollgaeth, since my wife is suffering from a most unpleasant geas, and I am told he is an expert at removing them. Also, I have a message for you and the King, but that had better be private.'

Maev rested her chin on her hand and surveyed him. 'Handsome man,' said she, 'it is easy to see that you are not much used to deceiving people. Your embroidery is in the style of Ulster, and now you will be telling me at once what this message is and from whom it comes there.'

'It doesn't come from there,' said Shea. 'It's true I have been in Ulster, in fact at Cuchulainn's house of Muirthemne. And the message is that your plan against him will bring disaster.'

King Ailill's fingers stopped their restless twitching and his mouth came open, while Maev's eyebrows formed a straight line. She said in a high voice, 'And who told you of the plans of the King of Connacht?'

Look out, said Shea to himself, *this is thin ice*. Aloud he said, 'Why, it's just that in my own country, I'm something of a magician, and I learned of it through spells.'

The tension appeared to relax. 'Magic,' said Maev.

'Handsome man, you have said a true word that this message should be private. We will hear more on it later. You will be at our table tonight, and there you will meet Ollgaeth. For the now, our son, Maine Mingor, will show you to a place.'

She waved her hand, and Maine Mingor, a somewhat younger edition of Maine mo Epert, stepped out of the group and beckoned them to follow him. At the door Belphebe giggled and said, 'Handsome man.'

Shea said, 'Listen . . .'

'That I did,' said Belphebe, 'and heard her say that the message should be private. You're going to need a geas as much as I do tonight.'

The rain had stopped, and the setting sun was shooting beams of gold and crimson through the low clouds. The horses had been tied to rings in the wall of the building, and Pete was waiting, with an expression of boredom. As Shea turned to follow Maine Mingor, he bumped into a tall, dark man, who was apparently waiting around for just that purpose.

'Is it a friend of Cuchulainn of Muirthemne you are now?' asked this individual, ominously.

'I've met him, but we're not intimates,' said Shea, 'Have you any special reason for asking?'

'I have that. He killed my father in his own house, he did. And I am thinking it is time he had one friend the less.' His hand went to his hilt.

Maine Mingor said, 'You will be leaving off with that, Lughaid. These people are messengers and under the protection of the Queen, my mother, so that if you touch them it will be both gods and men you must deal with.'

'We will talk of this later, Mac Shea dear,' said Lughaid, and turned back to the palace.

Belphebe said, 'I like that not.'

Shea said, 'Darling, I still know how to fence. and they don't.'

Fourteen

Dinner followed a pattern only slightly different from that at Muirthemne, with Maev and Ailill sitting on a dais facing each other across a small table. Shea and Belphebe were not given places so lofty as they had been at Cuchulainn's board, but this was partly compensated for by the presence of Ollgaeth the druid just across the board.

Only partly, however; it became quite clear that Ollgaeth – a big, stoutish man with a mass of white hair and beard – was one of those people who pretend to ask questions only in order to trigger themselves off on remarks of their own. He inquired about Shea's previous magical experience, and let him just barely touch on the illusions he had encountered in the Finnish Kalevala before taking off.

'Ah, now you would be thinking that was a great rare thing to see, would you not?' he said, and gulped at barley beer, 'Now let me tell you, handsome man, that of all the places in the world, Connacht produces the greatest illusions and the most beautiful. I remember, I do, the time when I was making a spell for Laerdach, for a better yield from his dun cow, and while I was in the middle of it, who should come past but his daughter, and she so beautiful that I stopped my chanting to look at her. Would you believe it now? The milk began to flow in a stream that would have drowned a man on horseback, and I had barely time to reverse the spell before it changed from illusion to reality and ravaged half a county.'

Shea said, 'Oh, I see. The chanting . . .'

Ollgaeth hurried on, 'And there is a hill behind the rath of Maev this very moment. It looks no different from any other, but it is a hill of great magic, being one of the hills of the Sidhe and a gateway to their kingdom.'

'Who . . .' began Shea, but the druid only raised his voice a trifle: 'Mostly now, they would be keeping the gateways closed. But on a night like tonight, a good druid, or even an ordinary one, might open the way.'

'Why tonight?' asked Belphebe from beside Shea.

'What other night would it be but the Lughnasadh? Was it not for that you would be coming here? No, I forget. Forgive an old man.' He smote his brow to emphasise the extent of his fault, 'Maine mo Epert was after telling me that it was myself you came to see, and you could have done no better. Come midnight when the moon is high, and I will be showing you the powers of Ollgaeth the druid.'

Shea said, 'As a matter of fact . . .' but Ollgaeth rushed past him with: 'I call to mind there was a man – what was his name? – had a geas on him that he would be seeing everything double. Now that was an illusion, and it was me he came to in his trouble. I . . .'

Shea was spared the revelation of what Ollgaeth had done in the case of the double vision by King Ailill's rapping on his table with the hilt of his knife and saying in his high voice, 'We will now be hearing from Ferchertne the bard, since this is the day of Lugh, and a festival.'

Serfs were whisking away the last of the food and benches were being moved to enlarge the space around Ferchertne. This was a youngish man with long hair and a lugubrious expression; he sat down on a stool with his harp, plucked a few melancholy twangs from the strings, and in a bumpish baritone launched into the epic of the 'Fate of the Children of Tuirenn'.

It wasn't very interesting, and the voice was definitely bad. Shea glanced around and saw Brodsky fidgeting every time the harpist missed a quantity or struck a false note. Everyone else seemed to be affected almost to the point of tears, however, even Ollgaeth. Finally Ferchertne's voice went up in an atrocious discord, and there was a violent snort.

The harp gave a twang and halted abruptly. Shea followed every eye in the room to the detective, who stared back belligerently.

'You would not be liking the music now, dear?' asked Maev, in a glacial voice.

'No, I wouldn't,' said Brodsky. 'If I couldn't do better that that, I'd turn myself in.'

'Better than that you shall do,' said Maev. 'Come forward, ugly man. Eiradh, you are to stand by this man with your sword, and if I signal you that he is less than the best, you are to bring me his head at once.'

'Hey!' cried Shea, and Brodsky: 'But I don't know the words.'

Protest was useless. He was grabbed by half a dozen pairs of hands and pushed forward beside the bard's seat. Eiradh, a tall, bearded man, pulled out his sword and stood behind the pair, a smile of pleasant anticipation on his face.

Brodsky looked around and then turned to the bard. 'Give a guy a break, will you?' he said, 'and go back over that last part till I catch the tune.'

Ferchertne strummed obediently, while Brodsky leaned close, humming until he got the rather simple air that carried the words of the ballad. Then he straightened up, gesturing with one hand towards the harpist, who struck a chord and began to sing:

'Take these heads unto thy breast, O Brian . . .'

Pete Brodsky's voice soared over his, strong and confident, with no definite syllables, but carrying the tune for Ferchertne's words as the harp itself never had. Shea, watching Queen Maev, saw her stiffen, and then, as the melancholy ballad rolled on, two big tears came out on her cheek. Ailill was crying, too, and some of the audience were openly sobbing. It was like a collective soap-opera binge.

The epic came to an end, Pete holding the high note after the harp had stopped. King Ailill lifted an arm and dried his streaming eyes on his sleeve, while Maev dried hers on her handkerchief. She said, 'You have done more than you promised, American serf. I have not enjoyed the "Fate of the Children" more in my memory. Give him a new tunic and a gold ring.' She stood up. 'And now, handsome man, we will be hearing your message. You will attend us while the others dance.'

As a pair of bagpipers stepped forward and gave a few preliminary howls on their instruments, Maev led the way through a door at the back, down the hall to a bedroom sumptuous by the standards that obtained here. There were rushlights against the wall, and a soldier on guard at the door.

Maev said, 'Indech! Poke up the fire, for it is cool the air is after the rain.'

The soldier jabbed the fire with a poker, leaned his spear against the door, and went out. Maev seemed in no hurry to come to business. She moved about the room restlessly.

'This,' she said, 'is the skull that belonged to Feradach mac Conchobar, that I killed in payment for the taking my dear Maine Morgor. See, I have had the eye-holes gilded.'

Her dress, which had been a bright red in the stronger illumination of the hall, was quite a deep crimson here, and clung closely to a figure that, while full, was unquestionably well shaped. She turned her head and one of the jewels in her coronet threw a red flash of light into Shea's eyes.

'Would you be having a drop of Spanish wine, now?'

Shea felt a little trickle of perspiration gather on his chest and run down, and wished he were back with Ollgaeth. The druid was verbose and hopelessly vain, but he had furnished the tipoff on that chanting. It was some kind of quantity control for the spells that went with it. 'Thanks,' he said.

Maev poured wine into a golden cup for him, more for herself, and sat down on a stool. 'Draw close beside me,' she said, 'for it is not right that we should be too much overheard. There. Now what is this of planning and disasters?'

Shea said, 'In my own country I am something of a magician, or druid as you call it. Through this I have learned that you're going to get all Cuchulainn's enemies together, then put a geas on him to make him fight them all at once.'

She looked at him from narrowed eyes. 'You know too much, handsome man,' she said, and there was a note of menace in her voice. 'And what is this of disasters?'

'Only that you better not. You will succeed against Cuchulainn, but it will end up in a war, in which you and your husband and most of your sons will be killed.'

She sipped, then stood up suddenly and began to pace the floor, moving like a crimson tide. Shea thought etiquette probably required him to get up, too, and he did so.

Not looking at him, Maev said, 'And you have been at Muirthemne . . . Which is to say you have told the Hound of what we hold in store for him . . . Which is to say that Cathbadh knows of it also . . . Ha!' She whirled with sudden panther-like grace and faced Shea. 'Tell me, handsome man, is it not true that Cathbadh sent you here to turn us from our purpose? Is not that tale of wars and disasters something he made up and put into your mouth?'

Seha said, 'No, it isn't. Honest. I did talk to Cathbadh, and he'd like to stop this chain reaction, but I came here for something quite different.'

She stamped. 'Do not be lying to me. I see it all. Cathbadh can no more protect Cuchulainn against the geas of Ollgaeth than a pig can climb trees, so he would be sending you here with your talk of magic.'

This was getting dangerous. Shea said, 'Cathbadh did admit that Ollgaeth was the better druid.'

'I thank him for the sending.' She turned and stepped across the room, opened a big jewel case, from which she took a gold bracelet. 'Come hither.'

Shea stepped over to her. She rolled up his sleeve and snapped the bracelet on his arm.

'Thanks,' said Shea, 'but I don't think I ought to accept . . .'

'And who are you to be saying what you will accept from Queen Maev? It is a thing decided, and I will never come to terms with Cuchulainn, no matter if it costs me my life and all. Come, now.'

She filled the wine cups again, took his hand, guided him to the stools and sat down close beside him. 'Since life will be so short we may as well have what we can out of it,' she said, drank off the cup and leaned back against him.

The thought leaped across his mind that if he moved aside and let this imperious and rather beautiful woman slip to the floor, she would probably have his head taken off. He put his arm around her in self-defence. She caught the hand and guided it to her bosom, then reached for the other hand and led it to her belt. 'The fastening is there,' she said.

The door opened and Maine mo Epert came in, followed by Belphebe.

'Mother and Queen . . .' began the young man, and stopped.

To give Maev due credit, she got to her feet with dignity and without apparent embarrassment. 'Will you be forever behaving as though you were just hatched from the shell, now?' she demanded.

'But I have a case against this woman. She made a promise to me, she did, and she has a geas on her that makes a man as ill as though bathed in venom.'

'You will be having Ollgaeth take it off, then,' said Maev.

' 'Tis the night of Lugh. Ollgaeth is not to be found.'

'Then you must even bed by yourself, then,' said Maev. She looked at Belphebe and her expression was rather sour.

'I think we had better be going along, too, Harold,' said Belphebe, sweetly.

Fifteen

When they were outside, Belphebe said, 'Tell me not. I know. She looked so fine in the red robe that you wished to help her take it off.'

Shea said, 'Honest, Belphebe, I . . .'

'Oh, spare me your plaints. I'm not the first wife to have a husband made of glass and breakable, nor will be the last. What is that you have on your arm?'

'Listen, Belphebe, if you'll only let me tell you . . .'

A form stepped out of the shadows into moonlight which revealed it as Ollgaeth. 'The hour is met if you would see the Hill of the Sidhe, Mac Shea,' he said.

'Want to come along, kid?' said Shea. 'This might be useful for both of us.'

'Not I,' said Belphebe. 'I'm for bed – geas and all.' She lifted a hand to stifle an imaginary yawn.

Shea said, 'Maybe I . . .' and stopped. He hated to leave Belphebe alone in her present mood, no matter how really unjustified it was. But it occurred to him that if he wanted to get any co-operation out of the vain druid, he would have to play along and butter him up. And it was distinctly important to learn about the system of magic here.

'All right,' he said. 'See you later, dear.'

He turned to follow Ollgaeth through the dark streets. The guards at the gate were awake, a tribute to Maev's management, but they passed the druid and his companion through readily enough. Ollgaeth, stumbling along the track, said, 'The Sidhe, now, they have the four great treasures of Ireland – Dagda's cauldron that will never let a man go foodless, the stone of Fal that strikes every man it is aimed at, Lugh's spear and Nuada's great man-slaying sword that is death to all before it but protection to the bearer.'

'Indeed,' said Shea. 'At the table you were saying . . .'

'Will you never let a man finish his tale?' said Ollgaeth. 'The way of it is this: The Sidhe themselves may not use the treasures – there is a geas on them that they can be handled only by a man of Milesian blood. Nor will they give them up, for fear the treasures may be used against them. And all who come into their land, they use hardly.'

'I should think . . .' began Shea.

'I do call to mind there was a man named Goll tried it,' said Ollgaeth. 'But the Sidhe cut off both his ears and fed them to the pigs, and he was never the same man after. Ah, it's a queer race they are, and a good man one must be to sit at table with them.'

The Hill of the Sidhe loomed in front of them.

'If you will look there carefully, handsome man,' said Ollgaeth, 'to the left of that little tree, you will see a darkish patch in the rocks. Let us move a little closer now.' They climbed the base of the hill. 'Now if you will be standing about here, watch the reflection of the moon on the spot there.'

Shea looked, moving his head from side to side, and made out a kind of reflection on the surface of the rock, not so definite and clear as it might be, more like that on a pond, wavering slightly with ripples. Clearly an area of high magical tension.

Ollgaeth said, 'It is not to everyone I would be showing this or even telling it, but you will be going back to your America, and it is as well for you to know that because of the spells the Sidhe themselves place on these gates, they may be opened without the use of the ancient tongue. Watch how.'

He raised his arms and began to chant:

'The chiefs of the voyage over the sea
By which the sons of Mil came . . .'

It was not very long, ending

'Who opens the gateway to Tir na n-Og?
Who but I, Ollgaeth the druid?'

He clapped his hands together sharply. The wavering reflection faded out and Shea saw nothing but blackness, as if he were looking into a tunnel in the side of the hill.

'Approach, approach,' said Ollgaeth. 'It is not like that the Sidhe will be dangerous against a druid as powerful as myself.'

Shea went nearer. Sure enough, he was looking down a tunnel that stretched some distance into blackness, with a faint light beyond. He put out a hand; it went into the hole where solid rock had been without resistance, except for a slight tingly feeling.

Shea asked, 'How long will it stay open?'

'Long enough for whatever passes to reach the other side.'

'Do you suppose I could open it, too?'

'Are you not a qualified magician, now? To be sure you could, if you will learn the spell. But you will give me something in exchange.'

'Certainly,' said Shea. He thought; there was the one he had used in Faerie. 'How about a spell to change water into wine? I can teach it to you first thing in the morning.' If he did it himself, the result would probably be rum of an uncommonly potent brew, but qualitative control was this guy's own business.

Ollgaeth's eyes almost glittered in the moonlight. 'That would be a thing to see, now. Raise your arms.'

He followed Ollgaeth through the spell a couple of times, then repeated it alone. The wavelike shimmering disappeared, and the tunnel came open.

'I am thinking,' said Ollgaeth, as they made their way back to the town, 'that it would be as well not to come here again the night. The Sidhe will be noticing their gate clap open and shut and setting a guard over it, and though they are poor in arms, it's a bad-tempered lot they are.'

'I'll be careful,' said Shea.

Within, he tapped at the door of the guesthouse.

'Who's there?' asked Belphebe's voice.

'It's me – Harold.'

The bolt slammed back, and the door opened to show her still fully dressed, a little line of worry in her forehead.

'My lord,' she said, 'I do pray your pardon for my angers. I do see now 'twas no more your fault than it was mine at Muirthemne. But we must be quick.'

'What do you mean?'

She was collecting their small amount of gear. 'Pete was here but now. We are in deadly danger, but more especially yourself. The Queen has given permission to this Lughaid who accosted you to take your head if he will.'

Shea put his hand on his sword. 'I'd like to see him try it.'

'Foolish man! He is not coming alone, but with a band – six, half a score. Come.' She pulled him towards the door.

'But where's Pete? We can't go back without him.'

'Nor can we go back at all if we do not live out the night,' she said, leading out into the dark, silent street. 'Pete is doing what he can to gain us time – his singing's wholly caught them. Hurry!'

'I don't see what good merely running away tonight will do us,' said Shea. 'Wait a minute, though. I can get in touch with Ollgaeth. You're right.'

There was only one guard at the gate, but he held his spear crosswise and said, 'I cannot be letting you out again the night. The Queen has sent word.'

Belphebe gave a little cry. Shea half-turned to see sparks of light dancing, back among the houses. Torches. He swung round again, bringing his sword out with a wheep, and without warning, drove a thrust at the guard's neck. The soldier jerked up his buckler just in time to catch Shea's point in the edge of the bronze decorations. Then he lowered his spear and drew it back for a jab.

Shea recovered, knocking the spear aside, but was unable to get around the shield for a return lunge. He thrust twice, feinting with the intention of driving home into an opening, but each time a slight movement of the buckler showed it would be futile. The soldier balanced, drew back for another thrust, and then swore as Belphebe, who had slipped past him, caught the butt end of the weapon.

He shouted, 'Ho! An alarm!'

They would have to work fast. Shea aimed a cut at the man's head, but he ducked, simultaneously releasing the spear into Belphebe's hands, who went tumbling backward as the man did a quick side-step and whipped out his sword.

Shea made a lightning estimate; the guard's face and neck were too small a target and too well protected by the shield, and the torso was doubly protected by shield and mail. Down.

He made a quick upward sweep that brought the buckler aloft, then drove the blade into the man's thigh, just above the knee and below the edge of the kilt. He felt the blade cleave meat; the man's leg buckled, spilling him to the ground in a clang of metal with a great groaning shout.

Behind them in the rath there were answering cries and the torchlight points turned. 'Come on!' cried Belphebe, and began to run. She still clutched the big spear, but was so light on her feet that it did not appear to matter. Shea, trying to keep up with his wife, heard more shouts behind him. 'The hill,' he gasped, and as he ran, was suddenly glad that the Irish of this period were not much with bows.

There were only occasional trees, but the moonlight was tricky and dubious. A glance backward showed the torchbearers had reached the gate and were beginning to spread. There ought to be just barely time if he could remember the spell correctly. Whatever dangers the country of the Sidhe held, they were less than those to be encountered by staying.

He was getting short of breath, though Belphebe beside him was running as lightly as ever. The hill loomed over them, dark now by reason of the movement of the moon.

'This way,' gasped Shea, and led up the uneven slope. There was the black rock, still shining queerly mirrorlike. Shea lifted his arms over his head and began to chant, panting for breath:

'The chiefs of the voyage – over the sea –
By which – the sons of Mil came . . .'

Behind, one of the pursuers set up a view-halloo. Out of the corner of his eye. Shea saw Belphebe whirl and balance the spear as though for throwing; he didn't have time to stop and tell her that such a weapon couldn't be used that way.

'Who but I, Harold mac Shea?' he finished, resoundingly. 'Come on.'

He dragged Belphebe towards the dimly seen black opening and then through it. As he entered the darkness he felt a tingling all over, as of a mild electric shock.

Then, abruptly, sunlight replaced moonlight. He and Belphebe were standing on the downward slope of another hill, like the one they had just entered. He had time to take in the fact that the landscape was similar to the one they had quitted, before something crashed down on the back of his head and knocked him unconscious.

Sixteen

Briun mac Smettra, King of the Sidhe of Connacht, leaned forward in his carven chair and looked at the prisoners, Harold Shea looked back at him as calmly as he could, although his hands were bound behind his back and his head was splitting. Briun was a tall, slender person with pale blond hair and blue eyes that seemed too big for his face. The rest of them were a delicate-looking people, clad with Hellenic simplicity in wrap-around tunics. Their furnishings seemed a point more primitive than those in the Ireland from which they had come – the building they were in had a central hearth with a smoke-hole instead of the fireplaces and chimneys he had seen there.

'It will do you no good at all to be going on like this,' said the King. 'So now it is nothing at all you must lose but your heads, for the black-hearted Connachta that you are.'

'But we're not Connachta!' said Shea. 'As I told you . . .'

A husky man with black hair said, 'They look like Gaels, they speak like Gaels, and they are dressed like Gaels.'

'And who should know better than Nera the champion, who was a Gael himself before he became one of us?' said the King.

'Now look here, King.' said Shea. 'We can prove we're not Gaels by teaching you things no Gael ever knew.'

'Can you now?' said Briun. 'And what sort of things would those be?'

Shea said, 'I think I can show your druids some new things about magic.'

Beside him Belphebe's clear voice seconded him. 'I can show you how to make a bow that will shoot – two hundred yards.'

Briun said, 'Now it is to be seen that you are full of foolish lies. It is well known that we already have the best druids in the world, and no bow will shoot that far. This now is just an excuse to have us feed you for a time until it is proved you are lying, which is something we can see without any proof being needed. You are to lose your heads.'

He made a gesture of dismissal and started to rise. The black-thatched Nera said, 'Let me . . .'

'Wait a minute!' cried Shea, desperately. 'This guy is a champion, isn't he? All right, how about it if I challenge him?'

The King sat down again and considered. 'Since you are to lose your head anyway,' he said, 'we may as well have some enjoyment out of it. But you are without armour.'

'Never use the stuff,' said Shea. 'Besides, if neither one of us has any, things will move faster.' He heard Belphebe gasp beside him, but did not turn his head.

'Ha, ha,' said Nera. 'Let him loose and I will be making him into pieces of fringe for your robe.'

Somebody released Shea and he stretched his arms and flexed his muscles to restore circulation. He was pushed rather roughly towards the door, where the Tuatha De Danaan were forming a ring, and a sword was thrust into his hand. It was one of the usual Irish blades, almost pointless and suitable mainly for cutting.

'Hey!' he said. 'I want my own sword, the one I had with me.'

Briun stared at him a moment out of pale, suspicious eyes. 'Bring the sword,' he said, and then called: 'Miach!'

The broadsword that Shea had ground down to as fine a point as possible was produced. A tall old man with white hair and beard that made him look like a nineteenth-century poet stepped forward.

'You are to be telling me if there is a geas on this blade,' said the King.

The druid took the blade and, holding it flat on both

palms, ran his nose along it, sniffing. He looked up. 'I do not find any smell of geas or magic about it,' he said, then lifted his nose like a hound towards Shea. 'But about this one there is certainly something that touches my profession.'

'It will not save him,' said Nera. 'Come and be killed, Gael.' He swung up his sword.

Shea just barely parried the downstroke. The man was strong as a horse, and had a good deal of skill in the use of his clumsy weapon. For several panting minutes the weapons clanged; Shea had to step back, and back again, and there were appreciative murmurs from the audience.

Finally, Nera, showing a certain shortness of breath and visibly growing restive, shouted, 'You juggling Greek!' took a step backward and wound up for a two-handed overhead cut, intended to beat down his oppenont's blade by sheer power. Instantly Shea executed the manoeuvre known as an advance-thrust – dangerous against a fencer, but hardly a barbarian like this. He hopped forward, right foot first, and shot his arm out straight. The point went right into Nera's chest.

Shea's intention was to jerk the blade loose with a twist to one side to avoid the downcoming slash. But the point stuck between his enemy's ribs, and, in the instant it failed to yield, Nera's blade, weakened and wavering, came down on Shea's left shoulder. He felt the sting of steel and in the same moment the sword came loose as Nera folded up wordlessly.

'You're hurt!' cried Belphebe. 'Let me loose!'

'Just a flesh wound,' said Shea. 'Do I win, King Briun?'

'Loose the woman,' said the fairy king, and tugged at his beard. 'Indeed, and you do. A great liar you may be, but you are also a hero and champion, and it is our rule that you take his place. You will be wanting his head for the pillars of the house you will have.'

'Listen, King,' said Shea. 'I don't want to be a champion, and I'm not a liar. I can prove it. And I've got obligations. I really come from a land as far from the land of the Gaels as it is from Tir na n-Og and, if I don't get back there soon, I'm going to be in trouble.'

'Miach!' called the King. 'Is it the truth he is telling?'

The druid stepped forward, said, 'Fetch me a bowl of water,' and when it was brought, instructed Shea to dip a finger in it. Then he made a few finger-passes, murmuring to himself, and looked up.

'It's of the opinion I am,' he said, 'that this Mac Shea has obligations elsewhere, and if he fails to fulfil them, a most unfavourable geas would come upon him.'

'We may as well be comfortable over a mug of beer in deciding these questions,' said the King. 'We command you to follow us.'

Belphebe had been dabbing at Shea's shoulder. Now she caught his hand and they went in together. The big sword was awkward, and they had taken his scabbard as well, but he clung to it anyway. When they were inside, and King Briun had seated himself again, he said, 'This is a hard case, and requires thinking, but before we give judgement, we must know what there is to know. Now, what is this of a new magic?'

'It's called sympathetic magic,' said Shea. 'I can show Miach how to do it, but I don't know the old tongue, so he'll have to help me. You see – I've been trying to get back to my own place, and I can't do it because of that.' He went on to explain about the court of Maev and Ailill, and the necessity of rescuing Pete and getting back with him. 'Now,' he said, 'if someone will give me a little clay or wax, I'll show you how sympathetic magic is done.'

Miach came forward and leaned over with interest, as someone brought a handful of damp clay to Shea, who placed it on a piece of wood and formed it into a rather crude and shapeless likeness of the seated King. 'I'm going to do a spell to make him rise,' said Shea, 'and I'm afraid the effect will be too heavy if you don't chant. So when I start moving with my hands, you sing.'

'It shall be done,' said Miach.

A verse or two of Shelley ought to make a good rising spell. Shea went over it in his head, then bent down and took hold of the piece of wood with one hand, while he murmured the words and with the other began to make the passes. He lifted the piece of wood. Miach's chant rose.

So did a shriek from the audience. Simultaneously an intolerable weight developed on Shea's arm, a crack zigzagged across the floor, and he half-turned his head in time to see that the royal palace and all its contents were going up like an elevator, already past the lower branches of the trees, with one óf the spectators clinging desperately to the doorsill by his finger-tips.

Shea stopped his passes and hastily began repeating the last line backward, lowering his piece of wood. The palace came down with a jar that sent things tumbling from the walls and piled the audience in a yelling heap. Miach looked dazed.

'I'm sorry,' began Shea. 'I . . .'

Patting his crown back into position, King Briun said, 'Is it ruining us entirely you would be?'

Miach said, 'O King, it is my opinion that this Mac Shea has done no more than was asked, and that this is a very beautiful and powerful magic.'

'And you could remove the geas on this woman and return the pair to their own place?'

'On the wings of the wild swan.'

'Then hear our judgement.' King Briun stretched forth a hand. 'It is the command of the gods on all of us to help others fulfil their obligations, and this we will do. Yet it is equally true that a doing should be met with a doing in reutrn, and this we cannot escape. Now, Mac Shea has killed our champion, and does not wish to take his place. There must be a balance against this, and we set it that it shall be this wonder-working bow of his wife's which if it is as good as his magic, will surely shoot holes through the walls of the mountains.'

He paused and Shea nodded. The man could be quite reasonable after all.

'Secondly,' Briun went on, 'there is the matter of removing his wife's geas. Against this we will place the teaching of this new magic to our druid. Now respecting the transfer of these two to their own country, there is no counterweight, and it is our judgement that it should be paid for by having Mac Shea undertake to rid us of the sinech, since it is so troublesome a monster and he is so great a champion and magician.'

'Just a minute,' said Shea. 'That doesn't help us find Pete or get him back, and we'll be in trouble if we don't. And we really ought to do something for Cuchulainn. Maev is going through with her plan against him.'

'We would most willingly help you in this matter, but you have no other prices to pay.'

Miach said, 'Yet there is a way to accomplish all they ask, save the matter of the man Pete, in the finding of whom I have no power.'

Briun said, 'You will be telling us about it, then.'

'Touching the geas,' said Miach. 'Since it is one that was imposed, and not a thing natural, it can be lifted at the place and in the presence of the druid who laid it, and it will be needful for me to accompany these two to the place where it was put on. Touching the sinech, it is so dreadful a monster than even Mac Shea will be hard put against it by his own strength. Therefore let us lend him the great invincible sword of Nuada, which is forbidden to us by its geas, but which he will be able to handle without trouble, at all. Then he can lend it to this hero Cuchulainn, who will make a mighty slaughter of the Connachta we detest, and as I will be with the sword and Mac Shea, I can see that it is returned.'

The King leaned his chin on one hand and frowned for a minute. Then he said, 'It is our command that this be done as you advise.'

Seventeen

Miach was an apt pupil. At the third try he succeeded in making a man he did not like break out in a series of beautiful yellow splotches, and he was so delighted with the result that he promised Shea for the hunting of the sinech not only the sword of Nuada, but the enchanted shoes of Iubdan, that would enable him to walk on water. He explained that the reason for the overcharge in Shea's magic was that the spells were in the wrong tongue; but, as the magic wouldn't work at all without a spell of some kind and Shea didn't have time to learn another language, this was not much help.

About the sinech itself he was more encouraging. He did a series of divinations with bowls of water and blackthorn twigs. Although Shea himself did not know enough of the magic of this continuum to make out anything but a confused and cloudy movement below the clear surface of the bowl, Miach assured him that in coming to this world of legendary Ireland, he had himself acquired a geas that would not allow his release until he had accomplished something that would alter the pattern of the continuum itself.

'Now tell me, Mac Shea,' he said, 'was it not so in the other lands you visited? For I see by my divinations that you have visited many.'

Shea, thinking of how he had helped break up the chapter of magicians in Faerie and rescued his wife from the Saracens of the *Orlando Furioso*, was forced to agree.

'It is just as I am telling you, for sure,' said Miach. 'And I am thinking that this geas has been with you since the day you were born without your ever knowing it. We all of us have them, we do, just as I have one that keeps me from eating pig's liver, and a good man it is that does not have trouble with his geasa.'

Belphebe looked up from the arrow she was shaping. Her bow was a success, but finding seasoned material from which to build shafts was a problem. 'Still, master druid,' she said, 'it is no less than a problem to us that we may return to our own place late, and without our friend Pete. For this would place us deeply in trouble.'

'Now I would not be worrying about that at all, at all,' said Miach. 'For the nature of a geas is that once it is accomplished, it gives you no more trouble at all. And the time you are spending in the country of the Sidhe will be no more than a minute in the time of your own land, so that you need not be troubling until you are back among the Gaels.'

'That's a break,' said Shea. 'Only I wish I could do something about Pete.'

'Unless I can see him, my divination will not work on him at all,' said Miach. 'And now I am thinking it is time for you to try the shoes. King Fergus of Rury was eat up by this same sinech because he did not know how to use them, or another pair like them.'

He accompanied Shea to one of the smaller lakes, not haunted by sinechs, and the latter stepped out cautiously from the shore. The shoes sank a little, forming a meniscus around them, but they seemed to give the lake-water beneath a jelly-like consistency just strong enough to support him. A regular walking motion failed to yield good results. He found he had to skate along and he knew that, if he tripped over a wave, the result would be unfortunate. The shoes would not keep the rest of him from breaking through the surface and, once submerged, would keep his head down. But he found he could work up quite a good speed and practised making hairpin turns until night put an end to the operation.

Next morning they went out in a procession to Loch Gara, the haunt of the monster, with King Briun, Belphebe, and the assorted warriors of the Tuatha De Danaan. The latter had spears, but they did not look as though they would be much help. Two or three of them fell out and sat under trees to compose poems, and the rest were a dreamy-eyed lot.

Miach murmured a druid spell, unwrapped the sword of Nuada, and handed it to Shea. It was better balanced than his own broadsword, coming down to a beautiful laurel-leaf point. As Shea swung it appreciatively, the blade began to ripple with light, as though there were some source of it within the steel itself.

He looked around. 'Look, King,' he said, 'I'm going to try to do this smart. If you'll cut down that small tree there, then hitch a rope to the top of that other tree beside it. We'll bend down the second tree . . .'

Under his direction the Tuatha did away with one tree and bent the other down by a rope running to the stump of the first. This rope continued on, Shea holding the rest of it in a coil. 'Ready?' he called.

'We are that,' said King Briun. Belphebe took up her shooting stance, with a row of arrows in the ground beside her.

Shea skated well out in the lake, paying out the rope, which dragged in the water behind him. The monster seemed in no hurry to put in an appearance.

'Hey!' called Shea. 'Where are you, sinech? Come on out, Loch Ness!'

As if in answer, the still surface of the lake broke like a shattered mirror some fifty yards away. Through the surface there appeared something black and rubbery, which vanished and appeared again, much closer. The sinech was moving towards him at a speed which did credit to its muscles.

Shea gripped the rope with both hands and shouted, 'Let her go!'

The little figures on shore moved around, and there was a tremendous tug on the rope. The men had untied the tackle, so that the bent tree sprang upright. The pull on the rope sent Shea skidding shoreward as though he were water-skiing behind a motorboat. An arrow went past him and then another. Shea began to slow down, then picked up again as a squad of King Briun's soldiers took hold of the rope and ran inland with it as fast as they could. His theory was that the sinech would ground, and in that condition could be dispatched by a combination of himself, the soldiers with spears, and Belphebe's arrows.

But the soldiers on the rope did not yank hard enough to take up all the slack before Shea slowed down almost to a stop. Still twenty yards from shore, he could see the sandy bottom below him, looking a mere yard down.

Behind him he heard the water boiling and swishing under the urge of the sinech's progress. Shea risked a glance over his shoulder to catch a glimpse of a creature somewhat like a mosasaur, with flippers along its sides. Just behind the pointed, lizard-like head that reared from the water, a pair of arrows projected. Another had driven into its cheek-bone, evidently aimed for the eye.

The instant of looking back brought Shea's foot into contact with a boulder that lay with perhaps an inch projecting from the surface. Over it and down he went, head first into the water of the marge. The sinech's jaws snapped like a closing bank-vault door on empty air, while Shea's head drove down until his face ploughed into the sand of the bottom. His eyes open under the water, he could see nothing but clouds of sand stirred up by the animal's passage. The water swished around him as the sinech came in contact with solid ground and threshed frantically in its efforts to make progress.

The shoes of Iubdan kept pulling Shea's feet up, but at last he bumped into the boulder he had stumbled over. His arms clawed its sides and his head came out of water with his legs scrambling after.

The sinech was still grounded, but not hopelessly so. It was making distinct progress towards Belphebe, who valiantly stood her ground, shooting arrow after arrow into the creature. The same glance told him that the spearmen of the Tuatha De Danaan had taken to their heels.

The monster, engrossed in Belphebe as its remaining

opponent, threw back its head for a locomotive hiss. Shea, skating towards it, saw her bend suddenly and seize up one of the abandoned spears to distract it from him. Tugging out the sword of Nuada, he aimed for the sinech's neck, just behind the head, where it lay half in and half out of water, the stiff mane standing up above Shea's head. As he drove towards the creature, the near eye picked him up and the head started to swivel back.

In his rush, he drove the sword in up to the hilt, hoping for the big artery.

The sinech writhed, throwing Shea back and ejecting the sword. There was a gush of blood so dark it looked black, the animal threw back its head and emitted a kind of mournful whistling roar of agony. Shea skated forward on his magical shoes for another shot, almost stumbling over the neck, but reaching down to grasp a bunch of mane in his left hand, and climbing aboard, cutting and stabbing.

The sinech threw back its head violently, it seemed to a height of thirty feet. Shea's grip on the mane was broken, and he was thrown through the air. All he could think of was that he must hang on to the sword. He had hardly formulated this thought before his behind struck the water with a terrific splash.

When he got his head out against the resistance of the shoes at the other end of his anatomy, the sinech was creaming the water with aimless writhings, its long head low on the bank, and its eyes already glassed. The sword of Nuada had lived up to its reputation for giving mortal wounds, all right. Shea had to develop a kind of side-winding dog paddle to carry him into shallow water past the throes of the subsiding monster.

Belphebe waded out to help Shea to his feet, regardless of the wet. She put both arms around him and gave him a quick, ardent kiss, which instantly doubled him over with cramps. Behind her the Sidhe were trickling out of the wood, headed by King Briun, looking dignified, and Miach, looking both amazed and pleased.

Shea said, 'There's your job. Do you think that lets me

out from under that geas you say I've got?'

Miach shook his head. 'I am thinking it will not. A rare fine change you have made in the land of the Sidhe, but it is to the land of men you belong, and there you must do what is to be done. So we will just be going along to see if you can avert the fate that hangs over this Cuchulainn.'

Eighteen

Shea and Belphebe were bouncing along in a chariot on the route from the section of Tir na n-Og corresponding to Connacht to the other-world equivalent of Muirthemne in Ulster. They had agreed with Miach, who was coming in another chariot, that this would be better than to re-enter as they had come and possibly have to fight their way through hostile Connacht, even though he was wearing the invincible sword of Nuada.

The country around seemed very similar to that from which they had come, though the buildings were generally poorer, and there were fewer of them. Indeed, none at all were in sight when they stopped at a furze-covered hill with a rocky outcrop near its base. Miach signalled his charioteer to draw up and said, 'Here stands another of the portals. You are to draw off a little while I cast my spell, as this is not one of the holy days and a magic of great power is required.'

From the chariot, Shea could see him tossing his arms aloft and catch an occasional word of the chant, which was in the old language. A blackness, which seemed to suck up all the light of the day, appeared around the outcrop, considerably larger than the tunnel Shea himself had opened. The charioteers got down to lead the horses, and they found themselves on the reverse slope, with Cuchulainn's stronghold of Muirthemne in the middle distance, smoke coming from its chimneys.

Shea said, 'That's queer. I thought Cuchulainn was at Emain Macha with the King, but it looks as though he came back.'

'By my thinking,' said Belphebe, 'he is most strangely set on having his own will and no other, so that not even the prophecy of death can drive him back.'

'I wouldn't . . .' began Shea, but was interrupted as a

horseman suddenly burst from a clump of trees to the right, and went galloping across the rolling ground toward Cuchulainn's stronghold.

Miach called from the other chariot, 'That will be a warden, now. I am thinking the fine man there is expecting company and is more than a little ready to receive it.'

They went down a slope into a depression where the fold of the ground and a screen of young trees on the opposite side hid the view of Muirthemne. As they climbed the slope, the charioteers reined in. Glancing ahead, Shea saw that the saplings and bushes on the crest had all been pulled down and woven into a tangle. At the same time a line of men jumped out of cover, with spears and shields ready.

One of them advanced on the travellers. 'Who might you be?' he demanded truculently, 'and for why are you here?'

Miach said, 'I am a druid of the Sidhe, and I am travelling with my friends to Muirthemne to remove a geas that lies on one of them.'

'You will not be doing that the day,' said the man. 'It is an order that no druids are to come nearer to Muirthemne than this line until himself has settled his differences with the Connachta.'

'Woe's me!' said Miach, then turned towards Shea. 'You will be seeing how your geas still rules. I am prevented from helping you at the one place where my help would be of avail.'

'Be off with you, now!' the man said and waved his spear.

Behind her hand, Belphebe said to Shea, 'Is this not very unlike them?'

Shea said, 'By George, you're right, kid! That isn't Cuchulainn's psychology at all.' He leaned towards the guard. 'Hey, you, who gave the order and why? Cuchulainn?'

The man said, 'I do not know by what right you are questioning me, but I will be telling you it was the Shamus.'

An inspiration struck Shea. 'You mean Pete, the American?'

'Who else?'

'We're the other Americans that were here before. Get him for us, will you? We can straighten this out. Tell him that Shea is here.'

The man looked at him suspiciously, then at Miach even more suspiciously. He pulled a little aside and consulted with one of his companions, who stuck his spear in the ground, laid the shield beside it, and trotted off towards Muirthemne.

Shea asked, 'How comes Pete to be giving orders around here?'

'Because it's the Shamus he is.'

Shea said, 'I recognise the title all right, but what I can't figure out is how Pete got away from Cruachain and got here to acquire it.'

He was saved from further speculation by the creaking of a rapidly driven chariot, which drew up on the other side of the hedge. From it descended a Pete Brodsky metamorphosed into something like the Connecticut Yankee at King Arthur's court. His disreputable trousers projected from beneath a brilliantly red tunic embroidered in gold; he had a kind of leather fillet around his head and a considerable growth of beard; and at his belt swung not one, but two obviously home-made blackjacks.

'Jeepers!' he said, 'am I glad to see you! It's all right, gang – let these guys through. They're part of my mob.'

Shea made room for him to climb in their chariot, and the spearmen fell back respectfully as Pete directed the driver through the winding gaps in the entanglement. When they had cleared it Shea asked, 'How did you get here, anyway?'

Pete said, 'It was a pushover. They had me singing until I almost busted a gut. I tried to get this Ollgaeth to send me back to Ohio, but he mixed it and said I'd have to throw in with their mob when they came over here to rub out Cuchulainn. Well, hell, I know what's going to happen to the guys in that racket. They're going to end up with their heads looking for the rest of them, and anyway I figure that if you go anywhere after you do your fadeout, it will be here. So one day when this Ollgaeth has me in the King's ice house showing me some of the flash, I figure it's a good chance to take along some presents. I let him have one on the conk, snatched everything I could and make a getaway.'

'You mean you stole Ailill's crown jewels?' asked Shea.

'Sure. I don't owe him nothing, do I? Well, when I get here, they roll out the carpet and send for Cuchulainn. Well, I give him a line about how this Maev mob is coming to hit him on the head, like I told him before, but I add that they're gonna put a geas on all his gang so they'll go to sleep and can't do any fighting. That was different, see? They all want to get into the act, but they can't figure what to do about it. I been watching this Ollgaeth, see, and the line I got is that if he can't get close enough, he can't make this geas business stick.'

'That's good magicology,' said Shea. 'Couldn't Cathbadh send you home?'

'Home? What do you mean, home? They told me to go to it, so I stashed the combination around the place like we done in the army. Then they made me head shamus of the force. Do you think I want to go back to Ohio and pound a beat?'

'Now, look here . . .' began Shea, but just then the gate of Muirthemne loomed over them, with Cuchulainn and Cathbadh beside it, accompanied by a tall, beautiful woman who must be Emer.

The hero said, 'It is glad to see you that I am, darlings. Your man is less beautiful than ever, but you will be handselling him to me, for I think that with his help I may escape the doom that has been predicted.'

Shea climbed down and helped Belphebe out of the chariot, 'Listen,' he said. 'Pete's already done all he can for you, and we don't dare go back to our own country without him.'

Pete said, 'Look, I'll write you a letter or something to put you in the clear. Leave a guy run his own racket, will you? This is my spot.'

'Nothing doing,' said Shea. 'Go ahead, Miach.'

The druid lifted his arms, mumbled one or two words, and lowered his arms again. 'The geas is still upon you, Mac Shea,' he said. 'I cannot.'

'Oh, I forgot,' said Shea, and pulled the sword from his belt. 'Here, Cuchulainn, this is the sword of Nuada. I borrowed it from the Sidhe for you, and it will have to go back to them after you're through with the Connachta, who ought to be here any minute. But it will protect you better than Pete could. Does that leave us square?'

'It does that,' said Cuchulainn, holding the great sword up admiringly. Light rippled and flowed along the blade.

'Now, Miach,' said Shea.

Miach lifted his arms. 'Hey, I don't want . . .' began Pete, as the chant rose.

Whoosh!

Shea, Belphebe, and Brodsky arrived with a rush of displaced air in the living room at Garaden, Ohio, and almost in a heap. Behind them, the door of Shea's study stood open. As the trio landed, a couple of heavy-set men with large feet turned startled faces, their hands full of Shea's papers.

'It's them!' said one.

The other said, 'And by gawd – Pete Brodsky, the synthetic harp, in a monkey suit!' They both began to laugh.

'Hell with that, you punks,' said Pete. 'I've had enough Ireland to last me. From now on it's *na zdorowie Polska!* See?'

Shea paid little attention. He was too busy kissing Belphebe.

And, don't miss Volumes one and two of this spectacular fantasy classic!

Volume 1

THE INCOMPLEAT ENCHANTER

IT COULDN'T HAPPEN . . .
A 20th Century scientist *couldn't* find himself hobnobbing with the gods of Norse myth . . .
You *can't* make a broomstick fly by chanting the right spell . . .
The beautiful girl you're chasing *doesn't* turn out to be made of snow . . .
Giants, enchanters, dragons, trolls, magical weapons and phantoms just *don't* exist . . .
No . . .?
BUT IT DID – in the first of the *Enchanter* books

0 7221 2930 0 £1.25

FICTION/FANTASY

Volume 2

THE CASTLE OF IRON

FORMULA FOR TROUBLE!

'All right, you guys,' said Harold Shea. 'Try not to interrupt me while I give a whirl at a sorites. If there is something, *c*, such that the proposition *phi* concerning *x* is true when *x* is *c* but not otherwise, and *c* has the property *phi*, the term satisfying the proposition *phi* concerning – .'
His voice trailed off, and he sat with lips moving. However, Shea's sorites was never completed. Through the domed building, far among the arches, rang the thunder of a cosmic voice – the kind of voice God might have used in telling the worshippers of the Golden Calf where to head in. It said: 'Oh, goodness gracious, I do believe I've made a mistake!' . . .

0 7221 2929 7 £1.25

FICTION/FANTASY